"GREETINGS [...] **PROPHET MILIA.** [...] **OF THE WAY?"**

Suddenly, everything clicked in Sonya Gomez's head. The odd sense of familiarity that had been nagging in the back of her head finally came into focus as soon as the serene Ferengi asked about "the Way."

"Yes," she said quickly, "we are."

"My Adjusters were concerned about your inquiries. Such questioning is not of the Way. Being part of the Way of Milia is to be of the whole of Milia." He nodded to them, putting his hand to his chest. *"Joy to you, friends. Peace and contentment will fill you."*

He faded as quickly as he'd appeared, the moment of confrontation having apparently passed. Gomez, however, felt her apprehension growing.

"We," she said, "are in big trouble."

STAR TREK®

S.C.E.

BOOK FOUR

NO SURRENDER

Mike Collins, Ian Edginton,
Robert Greenberger, Glenn Hauman,
and Jeff Mariotte

Based upon STAR TREK® and
STAR TREK: THE NEXT GENERATION®
created by Gene Roddenberry,
and STAR TREK: DEEP SPACE NINE®
created by Rick Berman & Michael Piller

POCKET BOOKS
New York London Toronto Sydney Singapore Evora

POCKET BOOKS, a division of Simon & Schuster, Inc.
1230 Avenue of the Americas, New York, NY 10020

Star Trek® S.C.E. #13: No Surrender copyright © 2002
by Paramount Pictures. All Rights Reserved.
Star Trek® S.C.E. #14: Caveat Emptor copyright © 2002
by Paramount Pictures. All Rights Reserved.
Star Trek® S.C.E. #15: Past Life copyright © 2002
by Paramount Pictures. All Rights Reserved.
Star Trek® S.C.E. #16: Oaths copyright © 2002
by Paramount Pictures. All Rights Reserved.

STAR TREK is a Registered Trademark of
Paramount Pictures.

This book is published by Pocket Books, a division of
Simon & Schuster, Inc., under exclusive license from
Paramount Pictures.

ISBN: 0-7434-6443-5

First Pocket Books paperback printing May 2003

10 9 8 7 6 5 4 3 2 1

POCKET and colophon are registered trademarks of
Simon & Schuster, Inc.

For information regarding special discounts for bulk purchases,
please contact Simon & Schuster Special Sales at
1-800-456-6798 or business@simonandschuster.com

Printed in the U.S.A.

These titles were previously published individually in
eBook format by Pocket Books.

CONTENTS

NO SURRENDER

Jeff Mariotte

CHAPTER
1

Deborah Bradford clutched Ben's small hand tightly as they boarded the shuttle on Kursican Primus. The boy had just turned three—big enough to walk on his own, but small enough that she was concerned about him getting trampled underfoot. She was especially concerned about some of the less humanoid races also boarding the ship—that Benzite, for example, whose bearing made him appear aloof, even haughty, might not have deigned to look down to notice someone whose head barely reached past his knees. Once they had taken their seats, though, she relaxed, as much as she could. The flight to the Plat—the Kursican Orbital Incarceration Platform—would take nine hours, the shuttle having been built more for load capacity than speed.

The Kursicans had apparently put little thought or effort into the passenger compartment of the shuttle. It held about one hundred and twenty seats, Deborah estimated, in four rows of three

seats each, separated by narrow aisles. The bulk-
heads were undecorated metal, and there were no
ports to show the view outside or anything else to
distract the eye. Passengers willing to pay a pre-
mium could ride in a private cabin, but there were
fewer than a dozen available, and Deborah hadn't
wanted to spend that much anyway. She just
hoped Ben would be able to sleep in his seat. She
wanted him rested and in a cheerful mood when
he met his grandfather.

Over the course of the nine-hour trip, he met
more of their fellow passengers than she did—not
surprising, since he was a rambunctious toddler,
and she was, as the mother of a three-year-old,
near exhaustion most of the time. Ben, though,
managed to make the acquaintance of Uree, a
Deltan diplomat on his way to the Plat on
Federation business; the Benzite, who turned out
to have a soft spot for children; and three of the
guards who kept wary eyes on the group. In the
aisle seat of their row sat a medical technician
named Isitov, a human from Val'Jon, which
shared this planetary system with Kursican and
Szylith. Isitov seemed glad of the distraction Ben
offered; Deborah had the impression that he was
nervous about this posting. But then he was very
young, and she was sure that even a more experienced sort might be a bit on edge about taking a
job on a space station that held one thousand
criminals—*well, criminals and political prisoners,*
she corrected herself mentally—with a staff of
only about one hundred.

She was most impressed that Ben had managed

to converse with Uree. The Deltan was part of a mission to consider the three sister planets for membership in the Federation. As a show of good faith, the Federation wanted prisoners from Federation-member planets to be released from the Plat and sent to Federation-approved facilities, or perhaps freed, if an examination of the facts proved them not guilty of the crimes for which they'd been imprisoned. Kursican had a reputation of being somewhat overzealous when it came to law enforcement, and the Plat had an even worse reputation as harsh and terrible punishment under any circumstances.

Deborah knew that seeing her father there would break her heart. But not seeing him would have been worse yet. Besides, she owed it to Augustus Bradford to introduce him to his first grandson, Benjamin.

After the shuttle docked in the Plat's shuttlebay, Deborah gathered her things and Ben's and prepared to disembark. Isitov stepped aside to let them pass, and managed to back into another passenger, dropping his own bag in the process. He scooped it up quickly with muttered apologies to the passenger behind him and to Deborah. She noticed a sheen of sweat glossing his upper lip as she stepped past him and toward the exit. *Poor guy really is nervous,* she thought. She held Ben's hand and led him off the shuttle, still thinking about Isitov because it was easier than thinking about her father, incarcerated for life because of his political beliefs. She hoped the trip wouldn't prove overly traumatic for any of them.

CHAPTER
2

Captain David Gold sat down behind his desk and ran a hand through his hair, thinking, *This is why it's so white*. He had nothing but respect for his crew, and he loved his ship. But the *da Vinci* bounced all over space like a pinball, it seemed. Anyplace there was a problem, he got the call. *Didn't every ship have an engineer or two on board?* he wondered. *Does S.C.E. have to handle every little thing?*

He knew that being indispensable was preferable to the alternative. But no sooner had they picked up Soloman, Carol Abramowitz, and Bart Faulwell from their sojourn on Keorga than Captain Montgomery Scott was sending them out on yet another emergency call. Gold had stepped off the bridge and into his ready room, because Scotty had specifically asked to speak with Gold in private. And, though he didn't yet know why, Gold knew that the only reason for that would be because there was something singularly unpleasant about this assignment.

"Screen on," he said when he felt ready to hear the news.

His viewscreen blinked on. In a moment, Scotty's face was before him. But the usually garrulous S.C.E. liaison wasn't wearing his typical smile. *"Good,"* he said, *"you're sittin' down."*

"Yes," Gold replied. "Why does that matter?"

"'Cause I'm sendin' you on a mission, even though the da Vinci *is the last ship in the fleet I'd send if I had any choice,"* Scott said.

"Where?"

"The Kursican system. More specifically, the Kursican Orbital Incarceration Platform."

Gold narrowed his eyes. "That's a prison station, no?"

"That's correct," Scotty confirmed. *"They're havin' a wee problem."*

"Why would you not want to send us? Not that I'm looking for a reason to go, but we're relatively close right now—and I stress 'relatively,' considering they're practically in the Delta Quadrant."

"That's why I am *sendin' you—time is definitely of the essence, and you're the closest S.C.E. crew I've got. As for why I would rather not—there's a personal reason."*

Gold didn't like the sound of that. But he knew the decision had been made. He paused long enough to tell Ensign Wong over the intercom to have the *da Vinci* change course for Kursican, warp nine. Then he turned back to Scotty's image on the viewscreen. "What's the nature of the 'wee problem'?" he asked.

"The prison—they call it the Plat—has gone com-

pletely haywire," Scotty explained. *"It's slipped its moorings. There's been no communicatin' with it, so they don't know what's happened. Its stabilizers are shot. It's spinnin' and bouncin' like a tennis ball in a tornado, the way I hear it, and its orbit is degrading rapidly. Somethin' isn't done soon, it's likely to enter Kursican atmosphere and slam into something. And there are a lot of folks on that planet—it'd be hard to drop a platform that big and not land on someone's head."*

"And the Kursicans are doing what?" Gold asked. "They can't bring it under control remotely?"

"They've tried. Between you and me, I don't think they've tried that hard. They seem not to care much about what happens to the folks onboard the platform—far as they're concerned, it's the dregs of Kursican and her sister planets. But when the thing comes down on them, they might sing a different tune."

"Still," Gold said. "It seems like they ought to make some effort on their own behalf. They're not even a Federation planet, for that matter. We're involved why, exactly?"

"You're right, they're not. But they're under consideration, and we happen to have an ambassador—name's Uree, a Deltan—who's out there now. In fact, he's on the Plat. That's our justification. We've asked the Kursicans if they mind us steppin' in, and they've given their blessing. If nothing else, we've got to see if we can get him off alive."

"Good," Gold said. "I'm starting to see the picture. One thing, though. Why not the *da Vinci?* What's this personal reason you spoke of?"

"Because, David," Scotty said, his voice somber, *"one of the prisoners on the Plat is a gentleman named Augustus Bradford. I believe you know him."*

Know him? Gold thought. *Now* there's *an understatement.* He hadn't heard the name in years, but he'd never forget it. . . .

David Gold and Gus Bradford had entered Starfleet Academy the same year. They had become close friends. After the Academy, they'd both served on the *Gettysburg,* under Captain Mark Jameson. Gus in particular had idolized Jameson, and Gold had to admit that, back then, the captain had seemed like the real thing. He was courageous, he was smart, he was not afraid of making hard decisions, and more often than not, he made the right ones. He was already justifiably famous in Starfleet for his negotiating skills, with his success on Mordan IV being the feather in his cap. When Gus heard they were being assigned to Jameson's ship, he had literally danced for joy.

But Jameson hadn't been quite the negotiator he had claimed to be. Decades later, the truth about what happened on Mordan IV had come out. Both Gold and Bradford had moved on by then; when the story spread, Gold had contacted Bradford and they'd spoken about it, and about the disgrace that had come to Jameson late in life.

Jameson had been dispatched to Mordan IV because Karnas, the son of an assassinated tribal leader there, had captured a starship and threatened to kill its passengers and crew unless Starfleet gave him the weapons he felt he needed

to avenge his father's death. Jameson got the
ship back intact, saving the lives of sixty-three
people, and he was hailed as a hero for his
efforts. But what Starfleet didn't know—until
years had passed and millions had died—was
that Jameson had given in to Karnas's demands.
He had given Karnas the weapons he wanted.
Knowing he'd violated the Prime Directive by
doing so, Jameson tried to fix things by giving
the planet's other tribes the same weapons he'd
given Karnas, thereby maintaining the balance
of power.

What he had really accomplished, though, was
to give Mordan IV the means with which to
destroy itself. A civil war began, which lasted for
forty years and came close to wiping out everyone on the planet. Decades later, now a retired
admiral, Jameson was brought back to Mordan
IV on board the *U.S.S. Enterprise*. Having taken a
restorative drug to counter the effects of the
Iverson's disease that wracked his body, Jameson
learned that Karnas had lured him back to the
planet to punish him for his long-ago actions. He
managed to negotiate a release for captive
Federation representatives by turning himself
over to Karnas. But it was already too late for
Jameson—the drug he had taken killed him, and,
at his wife's request, he was buried on Mordan
IV.

Gus had been different after that. Gold had
always stayed in touch with him—he had been
Bradford's best man when he married Anita, and
Bradford had stepped into a synagogue for his

first time when Gold had wed the lovely Rabbi
Rachel Gilman. Gold had become godfather to the
Bradfords' daughter Deborah, and the two families had often socialized and even traveled
together. But learning of Jameson's betrayal of his
principles, and his forty-year concealment of his
crimes, had turned Gus sour somehow. It was as
if, having idolized the man so much, he couldn't
deal with the truth about him. That conversation
twelve years ago, on hearing the news of Jameson's
death, had been the last time they'd spoken. All
of Gold's later attempts to contact him had been
rebuffed. Gus had left Starfleet, even left Anita.
The last Gold had heard, through the grape-
vine, he'd moved out of Federation space alto-
gether.

Which meant it was perfectly plausible that
he'd ended up in the Kursican system, Gold realized. He also realized that Scotty was looking at
him questioningly. "Sorry," he said. "A little remi-
niscence."

*"I understand, David. I'm sorry to have to spring
this on you."*

"No, it's not a problem," Gold said.

"Glad to hear it."

"Do you happen to know what he's in for?"

*"There's a political movement, mostly centered
around humans who settled on the planet Val'Jon,
opposed to Kursican or the other planets in the system joining the Federation. Apparently they went
beyond polite disagreement to violent action.
Kursican authorities rounded up the ringleaders,
and Bradford was one of them."*

"Well, that sounds right," Gold said. "He went there to get away from the Federation, after all."

"So I've heard."

"Don't worry about me, Scotty," Gold assured him. "I liked Gus Bradford once. But that was long ago, and there's a lot of water under that particular bridge."

"All right, then," Scotty said. *"There's one more thing you ought to know, though."*

"What's this, the other shoe?"

"More or less. Someone else is on the station—just went there to visit her father, according to Kursican authorities—arriving on the same shuttle as the Federation ambassador."

"Not Deborah," Gold said, remembering the brown-haired little girl who used to climb on his knee and beg for stories.

"Aye. Deborah. And her son Benjamin," Scotty confirmed.

"Gus Bradford is a grandfather?"

"These things happen," Scotty said. *"You ought to know that better than most."*

Gold glanced at an array of images phasing in and out of visibility on his desk in random order. Family photos. Scotty was right, of course—Ruth, one of his many granddaughters, was about to provide him with the latest in an even larger number of great-grandchildren. The only thing surprising about Bradford having a grandchild was that Gold hadn't heard about it. "I suppose they do. No matter, Scotty. We're on our way. We'll keep the thing in space where it belongs, and we'll rescue anyone on board that we can. Whether or not their name is Bradford."

"I know you will, David. I just wanted you to be warned before you got into it."

"I appreciate it, Scotty," Gold said.

Scott signed off then. Gold immediately went to the bridge. Just now, he didn't want to be alone with his thoughts.

CHAPTER
3

Commander Sonya Gomez and Lieutenant Commander Kieran Duffy studied the schematics of the Orbital Incarceration Platform that the Kursicans had—somewhat reluctantly, it seemed to Kieran—supplied them. They sat close together in the ship's briefing room, knees touching. Every now and then one of them would take the other's hand to point out something, and would hold that hand just a little longer than was absolutely necessary.

"It used to be a jumping-off station, early on," Sonya was saying. "They had the hardest time launching anything big enough for serious exploration from the planetary surface. So all their early launches were from the platform."

"Guess they didn't have the right inspiration," Kieran replied.

"What do you mean? Like what?"

He smiled at her, wishing there was time to lose himself in those deep brown eyes. "If they'd known you were waiting out there, I'm sure they'd have figured things out a lot sooner."

She laughed, a little uneasily, Kieran thought, and shook her head, then finger-combed strands of thick black hair away from her eyes. "Yeah, me and Helen of Troy," she said. "The face that launched a thousand starships."

"Exactly."

"Flatterer."

"I only say what I mean."

"Sure you do," she said. "Come on, there's a lot to cover here. What've you found out?"

Kieran breathed a long sigh. *Back to work,* he thought. *Sonnie sure has a way of getting down to business when she wants to.* "Like you say, it's old," he said. "Fairly primitive. The prisoners are kept here, in the middle." He pointed to a conical section—wide at the top, narrowing at the bottom—wrapped around a center core. "They're in stacked cells through here, the cells ringing the central passageways. Guards move through the core passageways, and they can see into or access any cell from there."

"How many prisoners does it hold?" Sonya asked him.

"A thousand," Kieran answered. "The worst of the worst, the Kursicans say. The ones they don't ever want to see again, I guess." He indicated a ring below the bottom of the cone. "Down here is where the guards' barracks are, between the cells and the support offices and operations facilities." His hand traveled down further. "This ring and corridor array is where ops is, all the prison authority offices, life-support systems, infirmary, mess, all that. Down here"—he pointed to the bottommost section of the station—"is a very closely regulated transporter room—"

"I would hope so," Sonya interjected. "Closely regulated, I mean."

"Right. Also, the power supply is down here. And the shuttlebay and escape pods are all here, too."

"So anyone who wants to get on or off has to go through there," she said.

"That's right. And the prisoners, I gather, go higher up the cone the nastier they are. Your everyday murderers are kept down low, near the bottom. Your mass murderers go higher up, with the lawyers and politicians."

Sonya laughed. He liked the sound of that, and the way her white teeth gleamed, pearlescent in the soft light from the display screen.

"Basically," he said, "we're looking at a small, floating city."

"Although not one you'd want to live in if you had a choice," Sonya commented.

"True. Especially now, since if you lived there you'd probably be having your head slammed against the walls of your cell every thirty seconds or so."

"Here's the tricky part, as I see it," Sonya said. "The station may be old, but the one thing they've kept up to date are the defensive systems."

"Makes sense. No point in having a prison station if just anyone can land on it and take away the prisoners."

"Right," she continued. "So when we get there, we can't simply beam ourselves onboard. We can't get too close without setting off phaser arrays, photon torpedoes, a whole range of defensive weapons. Even if we could bypass those, can you imagine trying to land in a shuttlebay that's spinning and whirling around in space with no set pattern?"

"I guess maybe we'll find out," Kieran said. He took her hands in his own. "You know, sitting here with you—even doing something as mundane as looking over the plans of a Kursican prison . . . there's just something about it that makes me want to—"

"Not here, not now." Captain David Gold stood in the doorway of the briefing room. "The Kursicans were very hesitant to even hand over those plans. I'd rather see you focused on them instead of each other."

Sonya stood quickly; Kieran could see her cheeks flush. "We were, Captain," she said. "I mean, we had just finished going over them again. I think we know as much as we're going to until we see the real thing."

"Good," Gold said. "Because we'll be there within the hour. Gomez, I'd like you to call your team together and let them know what they're up against. I wish I could go with you, but that's only for personal reasons. My place is here, on the *da Vinci*. You'll be heading up the away team, Gomez. Take whoever you need, but get on that station and restore its controls."

"We'll definitely need Elizabeth," Sonya said. Elizabeth Lense was the ship's chief medical officer.

"Emmett and the other medical crew will be on standby here on the ship," Gold said. "Once the systems are back on-line over there, those with the worst injuries can be beamed here to sickbay. There are likely to be a lot of injuries on that station. Most likely a good number of fatalities, too, I'm afraid. It's been flailing around out there for hours and hours at this point."

"Very well, sir," Sonya said. "I'll call a meeting and brief them right away."

"I think that would be an excellent idea," Gold said. "And you might think about sitting on opposite sides of the table when the meeting takes place."

Kieran shuddered as Gold left the observation lounge.

"What?" Sonya asked.

"Sorry, just had flashbacks to my father yelling at me when I was a teenager."

Gold had mixed feelings about the relationship between Gomez and Duffy. On the one hand, he firmly approved of being in love, if love it was. He certainly loved Rachel with all his heart. But on the other hand, he didn't serve aboard starship with Rachel. He missed her while he was away and she was home in New York. But he didn't have to worry, every time he went into action, where she was or if she would be harmed. He was afraid that if these two got too involved, there was always the chance that they'd be watching out for each other to the detriment of themselves, or the rest of the crew.

They were both professionals, he knew. They'd

proven themselves over and over again, under every type of circumstance. There was nothing they couldn't handle. In fact, when Security Chief Corsi had raised her own objections to the romance, Gold had defended their right to pursue the relationship, as long as it didn't interfere with their duties.

That was the problem, of course—shipboard romances could cause all sorts of *tsuris*. The same concerns went, he supposed, for close shipboard friendships, even when there was no romantic element involved. He and Gus Bradford had been that way for a while. They'd watched each other's backs, tended each other's wounds. Along the way they'd come to know each other as well, Gold thought, as two people could.

He found that part of him was looking forward to seeing Gus. In spite of the man's terse dismissal of him twelve years ago, and his refusal to talk to Gold since, he found Gus an enjoyable man to spend time with, and figured that probably hadn't changed. He was an articulate and creative man, a kind of philosopher. He was always thinking, always seeking, investigating new spiritual or intellectual paths. When he had an idea, he clung to it with bulldog tenacity. "No surrender" was his motto in his arguments with Gold. He would argue until he was blue in the face, but it always came down to, "No surrender, Gold. No surrender." Until the next new idea came around, at least.

He wondered if it was that stubborn streak that had landed Gus on the Plat. He'd find out soon enough, he guessed.

CHAPTER
4

Sonya had chosen an away team consisting of Duffy, Lense Soloman, P8 Blue, and Stevens. Domenica Corsi would head up the security contingent, accompanied by Drew, Hawkins, and Frnats.

Sonya had gathered them all in the briefing room and showed them the station's layout. Another viewscreen showed the prison platform itself, since they were now within visual range.

"That's a prison," Corsi said, belaboring the obvious. As usual, Core-Breach's blonde hair was pulled back into a bun so tight Sonya was afraid the security chief's skin would tear if she cracked a smile. "And we don't know what conditions are like inside. So my people go in first."

"Our initial problem is getting in at all," Sonya reminded her. "The Kursican authorities can't—or won't—tell us the modulation frequencies of the defensive shields, so we can't beam in." She had already outlined the impossibility of landing a shuttle, and the defensive weapons they would encounter if they took the *da Vinci* in too close. "There are more than a thousand beings on that space station, including a Federation diplomat, prison workers, and families of prisoners, and they're most certainly getting the stuffing beaten out of them, so we *will* get onboard and we *will* restore system functionality."

"I'll have sickbay ready to receive whatever we can take," Elizabeth Lense said, watching the station spin and flop in space. "Hopefully there'll be some medical staff there as well, and if their infirmary is in any kind of shape at all, we might decide to bring staff over. Casualties are likely to be in the hundred-percent range."

"One would have to be strapped in pretty tight in order to *not* be injured," Sonya agreed. "And even then, we're likely to see the most extreme cases of motion sickness in the history of the universe."

"Is it too late to back out of this one?" Fabian Stevens asked, a half-smile on his face. "Because seeing that much vomit is bound to upset my stomach."

"Much too late, Fabian," Sonya replied. "Just bring a scented hankie. And an entrenching tool."

Stevens made a face, but kept his mouth shut, which was the result Sonya had been aiming for.

"What about getting onto the station?" Vance Hawkins asked. "Given all the difficulties you've outlined for us."

Sonya turned to Kieran, sitting beside her in spite of Captain Gold's recommendation. "Mr. Duffy and I have been working on that, and we've come up with a plan."

Kieran had been waiting for his cue. "Here's what we'll do. . . ."

Fabian Stevens had only been half-joking in the meeting. Now, floating through space in an environmental suit, watching the surface of the prison platform slip past the windows of his helmet, he felt his stomach lurch. Conventional wisdom said to focus on a fixed point when in zero-g conditions to avoid space sickness, but the way the platform spun, there were no fixed points to be had.

He had to admit that the plan Duffy and Gomez had thought of was a good one—simple, like the best ideas were, and, so far at least, effective. The away team had been transported, in environmental suits, into space near the runaway station. The theory was that individuals would be too small to set off the automated defense mechanisms, and could make their way to access hatches and get inside. The transporter had dispersed them across a fairly wide range so that the automated systems didn't read the lot of them as one object, which meant some would have to travel farther than others across the platform's surface. But with the magnetic boots of their environmental suits, that shouldn't be too much of a problem.

He was currently less than three meters from the platform, and closing. It was the closing part that was a little intimidating—the platform hurtled past his face at an incredible speed. Making contact was going to be somewhat like jumping out of a moving vehicle at top speed, earthside.

Which, he thought, *isn't something I'd ordinarily do by choice.*

As he rushed toward impact, he heard Corsi's voice, via communicator. She didn't sound happy. *"Ooof! Watch out for the—"*

Then he was there, reaching out with his gloved hands for a protrusion that looked like a good handhold. It rose past his helmet, but he managed to get a grip on it with one hand. With his other, he touched the button on the control panel on his left thigh to activate the magnetic boots. His body rammed into the station, the shock absorbed only partly by his suit and mostly by his own skeleton, which would, he was sure, ache in the morning. But his magnetized feet came into solid contact with the platform's skin, and he let go of the protrusion, the purpose of which was still uncertain. Standing, he felt somewhat better. He knew that he was still spinning and flipping around in space, but he was moving *with* his main visual reference instead of in opposition to it.

"—the landing," Corsi continued.

A little late, Fabian thought.

But no later than he remembered what that protrusion he'd been clinging to had to be. A panel slid back, and he realized he was looking into a phaser weapon. He stepped backward as quickly as he could—the magnetic boots made diving out of the way an impossibility—as the phaser blasted into empty space.

"Watch for those squarish lumps!" he said into his communicator. "They're phasers."

"You mean the ones we talked about in the brief-ing?" Corsi came back.

"Yeah. They don't look quite like I expected them to."

"Just assume that every square inch of this thing is a weapon," Sonya's voice suggested. *"I don't even know that the Kursicans are aware precisely how well-armed this thing is."*

Fabian looked at the surface beneath his feet. Sonya's advice made sense, but at the same time, the platform was old, its outer skin pitted and charred. He doubted whether it could be as sophisticated as the commander speculated.

But on the other hand, it was old enough that there could be booby traps that none of the *da Vinci* crew had ever encountered before. It wouldn't hurt to step lightly—magnetic boots willing.

Looking across at the other members of the away team, he saw that they were following the same advice. A couple of others had inadvertently set off the hidden phasers. Probably a simple sensor set into the hatch that detected the presence of an intruder, he knew. Crude, but no doubt effective.

He started working his way, with the others, toward the bottom of the main core, where they had decided to go in. Corsi had worked her way to the front of the group already. He expected no less from the chief of security and his one-time—and he *did* mean one time—lover. She would always put herself in harm's way to protect the rest of the crew. He was near the back of the pack, as it turned out. Everyone looked pretty much alike in their space suits, especially with their backs turned—with the exception of Pattie Blue, who didn't require a suit—but he thought he was following Dr. Lense and Kieran Duffy.

He found out he was right when Kieran turned around to look his way. He pointed to a panel on the platform's surface—it looked almost like the rest of the thing's skin, but not quite as old and worn, less than a meter square. *"Look out for that,"* Kieran warned him over the comlink.

"Right," Fabian said, remembering this one from the briefing. It was a magnetic field that would reverse the polarity of his boots if he stepped on it, propelling him out into space. Since these environmental suits had internal thrusters, he'd be able to reverse course and return, but it still wouldn't be a pleasant sensation. This station was so old, though, that it had probably been built in the days before thrusters became common on environmental suits.

"Microtorpedo launcher," Corsi's voice reported. Fabian looked up to where she was—really, he supposed, *down* to where she was, since they were working their way toward what was supposed to be the bottom of the thing. But since it whipped around, out of control, there was no real telling what was up and what wasn't. He saw where she was pointing, though—an array of narrow tubes through which the torpedoes would fly if they were triggered.

In this fashion, each one pointing out hazards to the others, they worked their way to the bottom of the core, where the shuttlebay was. Commander Gomez had decided that was their likeliest entry point from the outside. It took twenty minutes for them all to reach the wide-open space. And when they got there, Fabian had a sense that the hard part was just about to begin.

CHAPTER
5

Gold watched the away team's progress on the forward viewscreen, though for minutes at a time they were out of sight due to the twists and turns of the platform. His responsibility weighed heavily on him at times like these—he knew those people were all in his charge, and while they were professionals, fully able to take care of themselves, in the end he was their captain and therefore would answer to himself—his own worst critic, according to Rachel—if anything happened to them.

Concern for their well-being, though, had to be balanced with the necessity of performing the task at hand. He'd been ordered to do this by Starfleet, and that was good enough for him. The fact that a one-time friend of his was on the careening space station entered into it, but not to a truly significant degree. Just as important as Gus Bradford—and Gus's daughter, his own goddaughter—were all the other lives, human and alien, at stake. Gold weighed the threat to his own crew against the certainty of death for all those people if action wasn't taken, and he knew what the answer had to be.

He remembered one of his many philosophical arguments with Gus back in their Academy days—an argument, he was sure in hindsight, that every single Academy cadet had at some point. They'd been walking, after dark, on the footpaths across the well-manicured Academy grounds. Crickets buzzed insistently around them and the occasional night-flying bird whisked by overhead. They'd been talking about the Prime Directive—Gus defending it in every instance, and Gold arguing for a more liberal interpretation.

"Imagine a planet," Gold finally said, "full of intelligent, creative, insightful beings. They're still developing as a society, but beginning to make great strides, in medical research especially. Within a few generations they'll make incredible progress, learning how to prevent thousands of diseases and plagues around the universe. Billions of lives will be saved because of their research."

"But of course, you can't know that they'll achieve this promise," Gus had interjected.

"Not at the present, no—you can only judge how advanced they are scientifically now, and estimate what they might be able to do in years to come. But they won't get that chance, because an enormous asteroid is on a collision course with the planet. When it hits, the near-total extinction of the race is a certainty. They've put their efforts into medicine, not interstellar travel. They have nowhere to go. We could save them—we could try

to evacuate them, or we could intercept the asteroid and destroy it, or push it off course. But that
would interfere with their 'normal development,'
according to you. So not only are *they* doomed,
but billions more across the galaxies, because they
will never achieve their potential. So tell me, how
is the Prime Directive beneficial here?"

Gus stopped on the path, hands on his hips. "It's
beneficial because it has to be applied with equal
fairness in all cases, David. If you choose to interfere because you like that race, and you think
they'll be useful someday, do you also choose to
save a vicious, warlike race from the same fate?
Perhaps they will turn out to be a bane on the universe, enslaving and murdering billions."

"Perhaps that's the chance you have to take to
save the good guys," Gold argued.

"No surrender, Gold," Gus said. "No surrender."

Which meant, in Gus's vocabulary, that the matter was closed, the argument over. It was infuriat-
ing, and yet somehow endearing at the same time.

He turned his attention back to the viewscreen,
listening to the away team via communicators.
Once they passed into the station, they'd be out of
touch behind the prison's still-functioning shields.

"We're into the shuttlebay," Sonya Gomez said.
"We're going inside now."

"Be careful," he replied, knowing she would
anyway.

"My middle name," she said simply.

"Don't believe her, sir," Duffy said. *"Her middle
name's Guadalupe."*

* * *

Sonya found the access hatchway from the shuttlebay, and then stepped back to let Corsi and her security contingent go in first. The Kursicans were basically humanoid in size and physique, though with orange, pebbled-looking skin, heads that came to fairly sharp points, and hands that consisted of three prehensile tail-like appendages instead of fingers. But the hatches and furnishings of the station would be of a size and design that would be comfortable to humans.

Corsi held a tricorder out in front of her as she passed through the hatch. Apparently the readings were satisfactory, because she disappeared into the interior, motioning for Drew, Hawkins, and Frnats to follow her. In a moment, Sonya heard Corsi's voice. *"It's an old-fashioned airlock,"* she said. *"Come on in, and we'll take the next step."*

One by one, the others on the away team filed through the hatch. Kieran tried to let her pass first, but Sonya firmly insisted that she bring up the rear. Kieran shrugged and went in. When Sonya followed, she sealed the hatch behind her. There was no light inside, so everyone turned on their helmet's overhead lamps, beams cutting this way and that through the gloom.

"The internal atmosphere is supposed to be within acceptable range for all of us," Sonya reminded the others. "All three inhabited planets in this system are close enough to Earth-like for human habitation, even though Val'Jon is the only one with a substantial human population. And most of the prisoners here—not all, but most—are from this system. But we don't know what the conditions are like inside, or even if the pressurizer will function in the airlock." She touched the control panel that would equalize pressure. "Let's find out."

A hissing sound emanated from hidden vents, followed by a greenish fog. Corsi kept her eyes trained on her tricorder's display, and when she spoke again there was urgency in her voice. *"That's poison gas, people,"* she said. *"Everyone's still got filters on, right?"* The others responded in the affirmative.

Fabian said, *"I don't understand—this stuff would be instantly fatal to Kursicans and everyone else who lives in this system."*

"It's another security measure," Hawkins suggested. *"So unauthorized visitors don't let themselves in. Maybe the airlock has to be operated from inside the station, or with some special code."*

"Code," Soloman repeated. *"Allow me."* He approached the control panel Sonya had used to fill the airlock with poisonous gas.

The Bynar floated before the panel—the airlock was still a zero-gravity environment—and began speaking to it in that strange, high-pitched computer language in which he was so fluent. Several minutes passed as he and the Kursican controls had an unintelligible dialogue. At the end of it, he touched the panel just as Sonya had.

She heard the hissing noise again, and the green fog dissipated. A moment later, Corsi announced, *"All clear. We're going inside."*

She opened the next hatchway and passed through. *"There's gravity, but the air's not breathable in here,"* she said. *"And is it ever a mess."*

CHAPTER
6

Lieutenant Commander Domenica Corsi stepped through the hatch into a place where artificial gravity worked and, therefore, the effects of the station's unbound careening through space were immediately evident in the beam of her headlamp. She had entered a kind of staging area, where prison staff would have suited up to make excursions into the weightless, airless space of the open shuttlebay. But everything was, to put it delicately, everywhere. Equipment, EVA suits, even instrument consoles had been uprooted by the g-forces of the station's motion, and were still flying across the large room with every new lurch the platform took.

And that included herself, now that she was inside the station's gravitational field. The station took a sudden tumble and she was thrown head over heels. No longer weightless, she slammed into the bulkhead with enough force to knock the wind out of her. Someone piled into her from behind, and she saw that the rest of the team was also bouncing around the chamber.

This is no good, she thought. She had scanned for any threats from other beings before even going through the hatch, and found the chamber uninhabited. But the motion of the platform could wipe out her whole team, just as surely as it must have killed the prison crew and inmates.

The room took another turn, and Corsi started to fall. She reactivated her magnetic boots, which she'd foolishly shut off upon stepping into the station's gravity field. She was on the floor, she realized, even though she was looking down at the ceiling. Some of the away team had fallen down there, and everyone looked a little dazed. P8 Blue had rolled into a ball, using her chitinous armor to shield herself. The others, though, were being battered. Corsi knew that the greatest danger here came not from the team being bounced around the station but from all the loose debris smashing into them. Even big pieces of furniture—tables and chairs and shelving units—that had been bolted down before had broken loose under the tremendous strain.

"Boots on, everyone. We have to get to ops!" she shouted over the comlink. "We have to bring the gyrostabilizers back on-line before this stuff kills us."

"Either that or cut the artificial gravity," Kieran Duffy replied. *"That would at least minimize the impact of everything being tossed around."*

"I'd rather restore stabilizers if we have that option," Gomez put in brusquely.

"Me, too," Duffy said. *"I'm only saying, if we can't, we have a backup plan."*

"Corsi, you remember the layout, right?" Gomez asked. *"We're not that far from the operations center."*

"I remember," Corsi replied. She at least had the advantage that she was standing on the floor—though upside-down, with the blood rushing to her head. This couldn't last too long, or she might have to drop to the ceiling and then work her way back up to the hatchway.

The station's next tumble, though, solved the problem for her. Suddenly she swung sideways. Now "down" was precisely the wall she wanted, the one with the hatchway in it. Instinctively putting her arms out to brace herself for the impact, she stepped down the vertical surface toward the hatch. "Let's go, people!" she called. "This is the way out!"

Corsi opened the hatch while the others followed suit from whichever surface they happened to be on. Everybody was able to grab a rail or a rung, and they started moving toward the hatchway. The difficulty came when the station continued its roll, and suddenly she was climbing up into the hatchway instead of simply sideways or down through it. Beyond the hatch, an empty corridor waited. She knew it led to the station's operations room and a command center, what would pass for a bridge on the antique space station. Either one would help, though operations was their preferred destination; from there it would be easiest to appraise the damage and assess how to proceed.

Corsi could see two hatchways ahead—above, just this moment, though she knew that would change—and she was sure that operations had been the one to the right. But for a moment she was not so sure which way was right. She wasn't moving along the floor of the corridor, she was sure—the floor was currently to her left side. Which meant, she deduced, that the hatch she wanted was the one that would be in front of her when she climbed up the corridor to it.

She really hated this whole deal.

Another few minutes and two shifts in perspective later, she managed to get the hatch into operations open. Something had fallen into it, she guessed, jamming it, and she'd had to use a P-38 to get the door open. When she finally did so, she was not at all surprised to see that the big space was full of massive pieces of equipment rolling and falling and bouncing like leaves in a strong wind. *Didn't these people secure anything?* she wondered. She scanned the room with her tricorder, finding no signs of life.

"Commander Gomez."

"What is it, Corsi?" Gomez asked.

"Please join me at this hatchway."

Gomez muttered her assent, and a moment later had slid down the corridor to squat at Corsi's side by the open hatch. *"I see,"* she said.

"There are no lifesigns in there. No security risk that I can determine—except for the incredibly obvious one."

"The equipment is pretty much smashed to smithereens." Corsi could hear Gomez sigh through

the comlink. *"Getting any of that repaired and functioning will be a challenge—especially since it'll mean dodging the big chunks."*

"Exactly."

"Do you think the command center will be in any better shape?"

"We can check, but considering what we've seen so far, I don't see any reason to think that it will be."

"If it's not significantly better, it does us no good. We can access the operations computers from there, but if they're utterly destroyed, we still need to get in here at some point."

"Your call, Commander," Corsi said.

They both watched a twisted, scorched chunk of metal that had once been part of an instrument panel flip past them, smashing into a wall beneath them.

Gomez shrugged and drew a phaser from a pocket of her environmental suit. Corsi understood what she was up to and did the same. They targeted the big pieces of wreckage, and within a few minutes had vaporized them. There would still be some danger from smaller bits of flying debris, but the danger was minimized.

"That worked," Corsi said.

"Thought it would."

"Are we going in or what, Sonnie?" Duffy asked from behind her.

"As soon as Commander Corsi clears us, we are," Gomez replied.

"It's all yours," Corsi said.

"There you go, Mr. Duffy. Happy?"

"As a clam, Commander Gomez," Duffy said.

Gomez started into the operations center, but Corsi grabbed her arm, stopping her. "One more thing," she said.

Gomez looked at her through their helmet windows. *"What is it?"*

"Do you realize what we *haven't* seen?"

"Anything right side up?"

"A living being. Or a dead one, for that matter. Nobody. There should have been someone on duty in ops, trying to restore equilibrium. I would have thought there'd be crew members in the corridor, or in the staging area by the shuttlebay. Someone, somewhere."

Gomez's brown eyes widened. *"You're right,"* she said. *"We haven't seen a soul."*

"I'm going to look around some more," Corsi said. "Hawkins, you stay here with Gomez, Duffy, Blue, and Soloman. Frnats, Drew, you and Stevens come with me and Lense. We'll go into command, maybe the infirmary, and see what we can find." Even as she made the decision, she questioned her own motivation for doing so. Why did she want to keep Stevens close to her?

"Makes sense to me," Gomez said, giving her approval.

"Stay in touch," Corsi said, gripping a wall rung as the station tipped again. "And the sooner you can get the floor to stay under our feet, the better I'll like it."

"Empty." Fabian's voice over the comlink was almost weary. This was the third place they'd

looked for life—the command center, the infirmary, and now the prison staff's mess hall had all been deserted. Progress from point to point was slow because of the incessant lurching of the platform, and Corsi felt like her stomach would never settle again. At least none of them had been sick yet, though, and Fabian's fears of encountering vast amounts of vomit had not been borne out— since there was no one around to get sick.

Still, she didn't like it. *This was a busy, populated prison station,* she thought. *So where is everybody?*

The ceiling she was walking on started to slip out from underneath her feet, and she latched onto a railing just in time.

And what's taking the engineers so long to restore the damn stabilizers?

CHAPTER
7

"*Progress?*" Sonya barked.

Kieran was concerned about her. Sonnie could be all business when she wanted to be, when it was important. But she'd been a little snappish since they'd arrived here. It was more than taking the job seriously—he respected that. But this seemed more like an unhealthy degree of tension revealing itself through her tone, well beyond anything demanded by professionalism.

He didn't like it—but he also knew that to ask her about it now, while she was exhibiting the behavior, would be asking to have his head bitten off. With Sonnie, you just had to know when to push and when to back off. In getting to know her as well as he did—getting romantically involved with her again—he had learned that lesson the hard way, more than once.

"*Most of this equipment is so old,*" Pattie's voice came back. "*I'm making progress, I think, but I still need some time.*" The bug-like Nasat had rolled herself into a ball and gone underneath one of the remaining consoles, where she was working on restoring the atmosphere on the station. Kieran didn't want to take the suit off until the gyrostabilizers were restored as well—it provided some cushioning for the inevitable falling objects and people—but he looked forward to being able to take it off and breathe normally again. The suit felt a bit claustrophobic after a while, and it had already been a while.

Soloman took a moment longer to reply, but the Bynar had been engaged in a verbal dialogue with the computer that controlled the stabilizers. *"There has been intentional sabotage,"* he said. *"Of a crude, but effective, nature."*

"Sabotage?" Sonnie echoed. *"How crude?"*

"A hammer, apparently," Soloman answered. *"Thrust through some primary processing units and wiggled around. Simple, but very efficient."*

"Surely the broken units can be bypassed," Sonya offered.

"That is what I'm attempting to do."

"Sorry," Sonnie said. *"Go back to it."*

Kieran was getting his hands dirty himself—figuratively speaking, since he hadn't been able to remove his gloves yet. He was on his back underneath yet another bank of computers that controlled the defensive systems. Unlike the others, he was trying to circumvent the computers, not repair them. These had somehow missed the original sabotage and avoided getting crushed by falling debris. But the control panels had been destroyed, so he needed to work them from the inside. He wanted to do the job without resorting to the old stick-a-hammer-through-and-wiggle-it-around technique. Though, if he didn't make progress soon, he would get around to that. Pattie was right; the stuff was so old it didn't seem to operate on any principles familiar to him. He had once had a friend who had collected personal computing devices—the very earliest ones of the late twentieth century. The technology he found himself faced with here reminded him of the guts of some of those very primitive devices he'd seen in his friend's collection. He wished he had dug around more in those early boxes.

Suddenly, though, he felt the station—which was beginning to tilt to his left—stop and turn back the other way. A moment later, it flattened out and remained in one position.

"I believe I have rerouted the signal successfully," Soloman announced. *"Gyrostabilizers are functioning properly."*

"Thank you, Soloman," Kieran breathed. "I am never going on another amusement park ride."

Pattie Blue made a tinkly noise that corresponded to a chuckle. *"This from the man who was flying all over Maeglin in his gravity boots. In any case, atmospheric conditions have been normalized. Breathable air and climate controls are on the way. Environmental suits should remain in service for two point seven minutes."*

Oh, the hell with it, Kieran thought. He, like every S.C.E. engineer, knew about Montgomery Scott's oft-repeated mantra—usually delivered in a full-throated scream. "Use the right tool for the job!" Kieran didn't have a hammer handy, but he had a manual door-opener in a pocket of his environmental suit. He pulled it out, jammed it into the works, and wiggled it around.

"Shields are down, Captain," Ina Mar said.

Captain Gold whirled to face the flame-haired Bajoran operations officer. "Scan the station, tell me what you see. *Da Vinci* to Gomez."

"Go ahead, Captain."

"Everything okay over there, Commander?"

"So far, sir," her voice came back. *"We've restored equilibrium, ceased orbital degradation, restored the atmosphere, and shut down the defensive systems. So we'll be able to beam the injured over to the* da Vinci. *Assuming, of course, that we find any,"* she added, sounding annoyed. *"So far the station seems to be deserted."*

"Ina, are there lifesigns aboard that station?" he asked. Ina nodded and pointed to a display screen.

"Yes, Captain. See?"

Gold swallowed. "Gomez, has the away team divided into two units?"

"Yes, sir," Sonya replied. *"Corsi, Lense, Frnats, Drew, and Stevens went off to see if they could locate the crew. They've been unsuccessful, and are returning to our position now."*

"Yes, I see that," Gold said. "I don't know about crew, but they're about to meet somebody. Several hundred somebodies, in fact."

"The prisoners, sir?" Sonya asked.

"That would be my guess. They're on an intercept course. Do you copy that, Corsi? You are about to encounter several hundred convicted criminals. They are to be considered armed and extremely dangerous."

Corsi replied, *"I hear you, sir. But if we've restored the necessary systems and prevented the station from dropping out of orbit, aren't we finished? Can't we all just be beamed back to the ship?"*

"No," Dr. Lense's voice broke in. *"There are most certainly large numbers of injuries on this station. We went through the infirmary, and it was deserted. Whether we treat the injuries here or there doesn't matter, but we need to provide medical assistance."*

"To a bunch of murderers and thieves?" Corsi asked. *"They're criminals, we're not allowing them aboard the* da Vinci.*"*

"They're sentient beings," Lense countered. *"They're entitled to treatment."*

"Not everyone on the Plat is a prisoner, Corsi," Gold said tersely. "Kindly keep that in mind."

"Yes, sir," Corsi said quickly.

"I'll relay the news to the Kursican authorities and ask for medical personnel from there," Gold said. "Though it'll probably take them a while to get to the station. In the meantime, be very careful with those prisoners. And if it looks like things are turning ugly, let us know and we'll beam you out immediately."

"Yes, sir," Corsi said.

Gold turned back to Ina. "Keep a close eye on them."

CHAPTER
8

"*We'll start making our way toward you, Corsi,*" Gomez said. Corsi and her team had opened the faceplates on their helmets to preserve the suits' air supply. The only drawback was that the air circulation system didn't seem to work very well—the station smelled rank, stale, and close.

"I don't think you should do that, Commander."

"*If you're about to encounter a few hundred murderers and thieves, as you call them, you might need some extra hands.*"

"And some extra guns," Corsi said. She and her part of the away team were making their way back toward the operations center, traveling along a corridor that they had previously covered every way but upright. "But if we're supposed to treat the injured, it wouldn't do to injure more of them, would it?" she added, shooting an annoyed look at Lense.

"In self-defense, Domenica, of course we would fire upon them," Lense said with a sigh. "But not if they aren't threatening us."

"Do you think maybe they've been baking cookies for us?"

"Most likely they're injured," Gomez's voice said. *"But like the captain said, be careful and assume they're dangerous."*

"I have them on my tricorder," Corsi said. "Looks like about two hundred life-forms. They're in the corridor that intersects this one, twenty meters from our position."

"Is there anyplace you can hide?" Gomez asked.

Corsi looked around. The last hatchway, into the infirmary, was a dozen meters back. "No place we can reach in time."

"Do what you have to do, then," Gomez said.

"Phasers ready," Corsi told her group. Frnats, Drew, and Fabian complied immediately. Lense didn't draw her weapon.

"On stun, I hope," the doctor said.

"Of course," Corsi replied. That was SOP.

Now they could hear the group of prisoners coming—the footfalls of hundreds, the rustle of fabric, the scrape of hands and shoulders along the walls. Corsi pressed herself against the corridor wall, for what little good that would do her in a firefight. Behind her, the others did the same. All of them—even Lense now, she was pleased to note—had phasers drawn and pointed toward the intersection.

For a split second, she regretted having told Gomez not to come to their aid. But against a couple hundred foes, what could five more do? Better to lean on their own abilities, and the knowledge that the *da Vinci* could whisk them away if things got out of hand.

Then there was no more time for second-guessing. The first of them rounded the corner and spotted them right off. The prisoners were a diverse mixture of races—a handful of humans, more Kursicans, numerous Szylithans, and various others. She recognized an Andorian, which surprised her way out here, and a handful of Klingons, one Breen, and some not so familiar.

The prisoners saw the phasers pointing at them and came to a stop. From behind, more came, jostling those in front. Corsi didn't know what to expect—she saw no weapons, but there were enough of them that they could overwhelm her little group through sheer numbers alone if they chose to.

The one in front—a Kursican with only one eye and a network of scars across the uneven orange flesh of his face—took a couple of steps forward. He started to lose his balance, catching himself on the wall.

"Help us . . ." he said plaintively. "Can you help us?"

Looking past him, Corsi realized that most of them were injured in some way—bruised and battered, red and green and magenta splotches of blood spattered here and there. Some of them limped or walked with crutches, broken bones showing through torn flesh. They were in no shape for a fight, she saw. She put away her phaser.

"You were right, Doctor," she admitted. "Let's get that infirmary up and running."

*   *   *

"Gomez to Gold."

Gold looked up from the fuel consumption report. "Go ahead."

Three hours had passed since contact had been made with the first group of prisoners. Nurse Sandy Wetzel and medical technician John Copper had been transported over to help Dr. Lense in the prison platform's infirmary—or what was left of it, anyway. More groups of prisoners had been located and some basic triage performed, with the most badly injured getting priority spots in line for treatment. Some were beamed to the *da Vinci* sickbay to be treated by Emmett, the Emergency Medical Hologram. Duffy, Frnats, Hawkins, Drew, Stevens, and Corsi had made a sweep of the prison levels and found numerous dead in addition to the injured. Gold had kept up to date as much as he'd been able.

"We've been taking roll over here, as it were," Gomez said.

"Still no prison staff?"

"No, sir. Only prisoners."

"How very odd."

"Yes, sir. Extremely. But there's one other thing that's odd, sir."

"What's that?"

"Either intact, wounded, or dead, every prisoner has been identified—except one."

Gold had a feeling he already knew where this was going, but she would tell it in her own way. Rachel had a brother like that—Joshua, a doctor back on Earth. He told great stories at family gatherings, but he withheld the punch lines for so long Gold wanted to throttle him sometimes.

"Sir, the missing prisoner is Augustus Bradford."

The Kursican Regent was named Aulyffke. The image on the *da Vinci* viewscreen was that of a squat, toad-like fellow with a voice like ground glass and skin almost as orange as a pumpkin. He sat in an oversized chair in an ornate room of his palace. At his side stood his Chief Magistrate, Juhstraffe. Behind them, extravagant draperies in shades of yellows and oranges clashed, to Gold's eyes, with their skin color.

For his part, Gold was flanked by Bart Faulwell, the *da Vinci*'s language and cryptography specialist, and Carol Abramowitz, the ship's cultural specialist. She had been briefing him for the past couple of hours on Kursican culture and mores, but the more he learned about them, the more he thought they sounded like an incredible race of jerks.

Aulyffke wasn't proving him wrong.

"You have lost the most heinous criminal on the Plat," he accused.

"Excuse me, Regent Aulyffke," Gold replied. Bart had coached him on the proper guttural translation of the name. "But I haven't 'lost' anybody. By the time we got here, the entire prison staff, our own ambassador, other visitors, and this one particular prisoner, were already gone."

Carol whispered in his ear. "I wouldn't stress the fact that they did nothing to help the situation," she reminded him. "He won't take it well."

Gold nodded—imperceptibly, he hoped, to the Kursicans.

"Nonetheless, you are there, close at hand, while we are here on our planet," Aulyffke went on. *"It seems like you would have more opportunity to find these missing individuals—most especially including the terrorist Bradford—than we do."*

"It seems to me," Gold argued, "that during the time it took us to get here, they could have gone anywhere. For all we know, they're right there on Kursican with you."

"They are not," Aulyffke insisted.

"Be that as it may," Gold said, "we have done what we came here to do, which was to restore control over the Orbital Platform. We're extending our mission to the point of providing medical care for the injured—though that is something that we would like the Kursican planetary government to take over as soon as is practical. In the meantime, a Federation ambassador and various visitors from Federation planets are still among the missing. We would like to know what steps are being taken to find them. I'll be here when you've made the necessary arrangements. Gold out."

The viewscreen went blank, and Gold turned to Carol Abramowitz, a pained look on his face. "Are they always so recalcitrant?"

"Pretty much, yes," the cultural specialist said with a wry smile. "The Kursican way, particularly among the governmental types, is to make demands on others, to take without giving, to expect to be served, and to have one's orders complied with unhesitatingly."

"Why do they want Federation membership?" Bart Faulwell asked. "It doesn't sound like they're really philosophically on the same wavelength as the Federation."

"It's primarily those same government types that want to become members. The Kursican system is a relatively small one, with only the three inhabited planets—Kursican herself, Szylith, and Val'Jon. Val'Jon was only settled in the recent past, after colonists from Earth moved out into space when warp drive became commonplace. They established a colony on Val'Jon, to which they gave the singularly unimaginative name of New Terra. The population of Kursican has exploded, to the point that they've been sending their own overflow to Val'Jon—not yet crowding the New Terrans, but it's obvious that within a few more generations they will."

"So is it the New Terrans who have applied to the Federation?" Bart asked.

"No, it's the Kursican government. Because their system is so small—even though their population has been expanding rapidly—they are trying to open up new markets. Apparently, their main motivation for Federation membership is financial—they think it will increase trade and provide new outlets for Kursican merchandise."

"Which it well might," Gold said. "Other planets have profited handsomely after joining the Federation."

"That's true," Carol said. "And it could happen again."

"But if that's their motivation, would the

Federation be likely to accept them?" Bart asked.

"I'm reading between the lines a bit," Carol explained. "That isn't what they're saying publicly. But it's what is at the root of their application, I believe. In this particular case, though, there's a lot of local sentiment against Federation membership. Because of the way the Kursicans tend to operate, the government, who made this decision, didn't consult any of the people who will have to live with it. The people aren't so sure it's in their best interests—and neither are the New Terrans, who left Earth in the first place largely because they wanted to try some different ways of life. Your friend, Captain, is one of the primary foes of Federation membership, and he's been a very vocal advocate for his cause. He was imprisoned basically as a way to shut him up, because he had been leading an increasingly noisy anti-Federation movement. The whole issue has become a flash-point now—if the government loses on this issue, they just might find themselves out of power."

"Which makes Gus just a political prisoner?" Gold asked. "Or has he committed any actual crimes?"

"Nothing we'd consider a crime," Carol replied. "He's led rallies, marches, made speeches. There has been some violence associated with some of the protests, but nothing directly attributable to Bradford. He was arrested on a fairly specious charge of 'inciting revolution,' which is hard to disprove because it is, in fact, revolutionary for the lower castes and the human colonists to disagree so vocally and publicly with the government's pronouncements."

"As I said," Gold insisted. "A political prisoner."

"And a missing political prisoner at that," Bart added.

CHAPTER
9

Sonya Gomez stood in the corridor outside the infirmary, arms crossed over her chest, phaser in hand. She was trying to look authoritative. These were still prisoners, after all. The hours they'd spent topsy-turvy had knocked the resistance out of them, for now, and they had meekly submitted to her crew's command. But she didn't expect that to last long, and had already had Corsi's security crew pull those with only minor injuries, or mere nausea from the ride, and return them to their cells.

At some point, she believed, the rest would try to overcome the comparatively few *da Vinci* crew members on board. Corsi had had five more of her people beam down, but it was still a drop in the bucket when you compared the numbers. She wasn't sure what would happen if the prisoners got unruly. Maintaining order on a Kursican prison station wasn't her responsibility. She could—and she was certain that Captain Gold would back her up on this—simply pull her crew off and turn the station over to the prisoners if it looked like they were becoming unruly. But she hoped that a little show of force would prevent things from getting to that point, and that the Kursican authorities would send a replacement staff as quickly as possible. To that end, she had decided that every member of her team who wasn't specifically involved in medical treatment or an engineering task should keep weapons visible at all times. Going along with that was the necessity of remaining alert—the last thing they needed was a prisoner getting his or her hands on one of their phasers.

Soloman approached her. Like the others, he had removed his environmental suit in order to move more freely, and his uniform was stained and torn in a couple of spots. He had been in and under and through nearly every component of the station's operations center during the course of the day. P8 Blue was keeping things running, while Soloman concentrated on repairing the damage that had been done and trying to figure out exactly what happened. Now he had an expectant look on his face.

"What is it, Soloman?" she asked.

"I've been working on re-creating the sequence of events that led to the damage to the station's systems, Commander," he said. "I've been able to access station logs, which have given me some information, and by working backward through the system failures, I've been able to determine the sequence of damages."

"And what have you found out?" she asked. Instead of looking directly at him, though, she looked past his head, toward the prisoners, making sure they could see that she remained armed and observant. A few meters down the hall was Drew, and Duffy beyond him, and where the line of prisoners awaiting treatment turned a corner, Hawkins was stationed.

"There were saboteurs in place on the station, presumably in crew positions," he said. "Security on the station was such that only crew members could possibly have had access to some of the more sensitive controls. Since those controls were accessed and altered, the only reasonable assumption is that some crew members were actually working for the opposition."

"Do we know who the opposition is?" Sonya asked.

"No, Commander. But we know what their goal was—to remove all the station's crew, any visitors, and the one prisoner, Augustus Bradford, from the station."

"So my guess would be that Bradford was the main target. They wanted to break him out."

"That's a reasonable guess."

"Go on," she said.

"The saboteurs disarmed the station's defenses and altered life-support systems, decreasing the amount of oxygen in the air. The saboteurs must have been equipped with artificial breathing devices, so they could maintain consciousness while everyone else who breathes oxygen—which includes all Kursican guards and crew and most of the prisoners—lost consciousness. With the guards dormant and defenses down, two shuttles approached the station, and the first one docked in the shuttlebay. Several humans came off that shuttle, heavily armed, but the saboteurs' efforts had already paid off and there was no resistance to them. They beamed the unconscious guards and staff onto the two shuttles—even the ones on duty in the cell blocks—and also located and transported Bradford.

"Once they were all on the shuttle—except one—that final saboteur reset the defense mechanisms to normal and wrecked the gyrostabilizer units and the atmospheric controls. Since he or she could no longer be transported off, he or she put on an environmental suit and went into the shuttlebay and left the station that way—just as we came on—and was beamed onto the shuttle once he or she was past the shields. That last part is an extrapolation, since by that point the station's logs were no longer recording," he added with an almost apologetic look, "but it's the only reasonable one to make, considering the evidence."

"So it's a safe bet that anyone who was involved in that plot is long gone—and the prisoners still here were not part of it."

"Yes, Commander."

"And not only that, but they slept through it—only waking up after we restored the oxygen levels."

"Yes, Commander."

"No wonder they're still kind of dazed. Thank

you, Soloman." She watched his departing form as he headed back to the operations center, his bulbous bald head and narrow frame catching the light. She thought he had recovered nicely from the loss of his bonded mate. Bynars were not supposed to function well as individuals, and she wasn't sure what his emotional state was really like, since he tended to keep that sort of thing to himself. But as a member of her crew, he was as worthwhile as they came, and she was glad he'd been willing to stick it out.

But the big question he hadn't been able to answer remained—what had become of the missing crew, and Augustus Bradford?

Augustus Bradford strode purposefully across the large room toward the communications system they'd set up at one end. He and his fellow fugitives from justice were ensconced in an industrial building in a remote outpost on Val'Jon, half a world away from the New Terran colony. Now they were truly fugitives, in that they'd gone from merely speaking out to actually committing an act that would be considered criminal by the Kursican authorities.

"Are you ready to make the call?" Malkety asked him. Malkety was a Kursican, but a sympathizer to the cause, a staunch opponent of Federation membership for the Kursican system.

"It's time," Bradford said, suppressing a scowl. "But only because Gold's ship messed with our timetable."

Augustus Bradford still cut an imposing figure,

as he once had on the bridge of a starship, though he was dressed in old, faded work clothing and his shock of red hair had mostly gone to white. His jaw was still firm, though, his eyes steely, his mouth a thin, determined line.

He had counted on the chaos aboard the Plat to disguise his disappearance for a couple of days at least, giving him time to get his plan into motion. And his plan was nothing less than an uprising: finally motivating the majority of citizens across the system—on Szylith, Val'Jon, and Kursican herself—to rise up, to throw off the yoke of Kursican authority, and to take their futures into their own hands. The groundwork had been painstakingly laid for months, waiting only for Bradford's triumphant return from the Plat to set it off.

But spreading the word of his return, and setting the wheels of revolution in motion, would take time. And time, apparently, was what he no longer had—thanks to his old friend, David Gold. "I owe you for this one, Gold," he muttered to himself. Then, turning back to Malkety, he composed himself and said, "Let's do this."

Malkety flipped a series of switches and nodded his head. Bradford looked into the screen. "Citizens of the Kursican System," he began, "and representatives of the corrupt so-called Kursican Planetary Government—you know who I am. I am Augustus Bradford of New Terra, formerly a political prisoner on the Kursican Orbital Incarceration Platform. But now I am a free man, thanks to the support of the vast majority of you. Not only do you know who I am, you know what I stand for. I stand for the self-rule of the Kursican system. I stand for an end to negotiations with some distant interplanetary Federation that does not really have our interests at heart. And I stand for the overthrow—armed, if necessary—of the outdated, unwanted, unnecessary Kursican Planetary Government. Your time, rulers of Kursican, is over. A new era is upon us, an era of self-rule—by the citizenry, for the citizenry.

"I have with me nearly a hundred prison guards and staff—tools of the corrupt government. We have offered them the opportunity to join our movement, and many of them have agreed, because they understand that they were used by an unjust system to oppress their fellows. Others, however, have declined to join us. I am sorry to say that unless the Aulyffke, Regent of Kursican, and his puppets step down from their posts within one Kursican day, these hostages will be killed. And that regrettable act will only be the first of many. Aulyffke, you will not survive another day and night, and neither will those who help you cling to power. Unless you step down, blood will flow. It is in your power to prevent this bloodshed. If you have any decency whatsoever, any love for the people you claim to represent, you will announce your abdication from power immediately.

"Additionally, all Federation personnel, including the Starship *da Vinci*, must leave the system at once, or risk being violently expelled.

"Bradford out."

Malkety shut down the broadcast instantly, lest the source be traced back to this forgotten outpost.

"How was that?" Bradford asked.

Around him, his people broke out in cheers.

CHAPTER
10

"Is that the Gus Bradford you remember?" Bart asked.

"Yes and no," Gold said. "He's every bit as stubborn as I remember him. But a good deal less sane, I would say."

"Well, yeah," Bart said. "I mean, he *was* a starship captain, right? He would have to have been more sane at some point. He sounds pretty much like a madman now."

They were in Gold's ready room, watching the recording for the third time with Carol and David McAllan, the ship's tactical officer. It had been broadcast all over the system, and Gold had relayed it on to Starfleet. The official response had been to stay and collect Ambassador Uree, after which the Kursicans could deal with their own problems. "Collecting" Uree could be tricky, though, since Gold had no idea where on the three planets Bradford and his hostages were.

But maybe the Kursicans did. . . .

"Get me Aulyffke," he said. A few moments later, the Kursican Regent appeared on the viewscreen.

"Yes, Captain Gold? I have a bit of an urgent situation developing here, as you are no doubt aware, so I cannot spare you much time."

"I don't need much time, Regent. I want to talk to Gus Bradford. Surely you have some way of contacting him to discuss his demands."

"He is a terrorist," the Regent said flatly. *"We will not negotiate with him."*

"I'm not asking you to; I'm simply asking if you know how to reach him."

"I am given to understand that he is an old friend of yours, Captain Gold," Aulyffke replied. *"How do I know you aren't working with him?"*

Gold shook his head wearily. "Because I represent the Federation that he hates?"

"This is true," Aulyffke granted.

"So, how about it?" Gold pressed. "How do I reach him?"

The Regent hemmed and hawed, then finally said, *"We not only know how to get in touch with him, Captain—we know where he is."*

Gold bit back a comment about how stunned he was that the Kursican government had actually managed to accomplish something on its own. "Good. Where?"

"A base in orbit around Val'Jon. And we plan to obliterate it."

"What!" Gold leaned forward. "You can't do that!"

"We do not negotiate with terrorists, Captain Gold," Aulyffke repeated. *"That is a cardinal rule. There are no exceptions."*

Gold's mind raced furiously. He pictured Deborah and little Ben—then pictured them being vaporized. "Give me an hour, Regent, please."

"To do what?"

"What you're not willing to do—save lives."

"Captain—"

"You may not negotiate with terrorists, but I've been ordered to save the lives of Ambassador Uree and the other two Federation citizens he's holding. Those orders came from the same Federation that you want to join, Regent."

The look on Aulyffke's face told Gold that he'd hit the right note. A negative report on the Kursican government's behavior would damage their application to the Federation, and the Regent did not want that.

"Very well, Captain Gold. One hour. After that, we destroy your friend Augustus Bradford and his cabal of agitators once and for all."

"Frnats overheard some talk among the prisoners," Corsi reported. "I don't like the sound of it."

"What kind of talk?" Sonya asked. She maintained her position outside the infirmary, where the line for treatment still stretched down the corridor and around a corner.

"You know," Corsi said. "There are only a few of us and a lot of them, they could get our phasers, even if a couple of them went down they'd still out-number us a hundred to one. That kind of thing."

"And they said this right in front of Frnats?"

"They don't get many Bolians around here, apparently," Corsi replied. "I don't know if they thought she couldn't understand them, or didn't know how keen her hearing is. The point is, what are we going to do about it?"

"What can we do?" Sonya asked. "They're right."

"Then we should get out of here."

"Not until they make a move, or we're ordered out by Captain Gold," Sonya said with finality. "I won't run because of a couple of grumbling mal-contents."

Corsi glared at her. "You haven't liked this assignment from the beginning, Commander," she said. "I'm surprised you're not willing to leave before the trouble starts."

"You're right, Commander," Sonya replied, clip-ping the words short. "I don't like it. But it's the job we've been assigned to do. Now, if there's noth-ing else?"

Corsi turned on her heel and walked away.

Sonya watched her go, knowing the security chief was right—the tension in the corridor was as sharp as a razor's edge, the air thick with the min-gled smells of sweat and fear. Something was going to happen soon. Her people just had to be ready when it did.

Ensign Wong turned to look at Captain Gold in his command chair. "We're in orbit around Val'Jon, sir."

"Pull within thirty thousand kilometers, and hold position."

"Yes, sir."

"Ina, try to raise Augustus Bradford. Tell him I want to talk to him privately."

The Bajoran nodded. "Aye, aye, sir."

Gold opened an intercom channel. "Transporter room. Feliciano, can you get a lock on anything in there?"

A few moments later, the transporter chief replied, *"No, sir. They're using the same kind of shield that the Plat uses."*

"And there's no way to get through it?"

"No, sir."

"I don't buy that. We're supposed to be the damn problem-solvers of the galaxy—so get on it, pronto! Get Barnak and anyone else you need from engineering to help out. You've got less than an hour to find a way to get those people out of there, Chief."

"We'll get on it right away, sir."

"Captain?"

Gold turned to the ops console. "Yes, Lieutenant?"

"I have Augustus Bradford, sir."

It felt like there was a rock in David Gold's stomach. "In my ready room, Ina."

"David Gold. Imagine that. After all these years, you're the one they send after me."

"I didn't come here for you, Gus," Gold said. He was alone in the ready room now. "And I don't care what mess you've gotten yourself into. I only want one thing."

"And what's that?"

"Ambassador Uree, Deborah, and Benjamin returned to me, safe and sound."

"They're all fine, David. You'll just have to take my word for it. But I can't release them to you. I'm surprised you'd think they weren't safe and sound, to be honest."

"I don't know you anymore, Gus. I don't know what you might do."

"I'm sorry that your estimation of me has sunk so low. We were friends, once upon a time."

"That was long ago, Gus. A lifetime ago."

"Lives are short, David."

"That depends on how you live them."

Bradford laughed, an explosive sound. *"I'll tell you, when I wore a Starfleet uniform, with my own ship, I felt like every day was a lifetime long. I've never felt as free as I have here on New Terra."*

"The Federation isn't as bad as you make it out to be, Gus."

"Nor is it as good as you'd like to think. You still wear the uniform. You've brainwashed yourself, David. You don't want to think that your life has been wasted in service of the wrong ideals."

Gold turned away from the viewscreen so Bradford couldn't see him trying not to laugh. When he had regained his composure, he turned back.

"The ideals I serve are the same ones you used to believe in, Gus. Decency, fairness, honor, duty. You remember our arguments, Gus? You were always the one defending the Federation against my challenges, my assaults.

Turns out the Federation is able to defend itself. It's not the intransigent monolith I believed it to be after all. Maybe it's time you took another look."

"No thanks, David." The look on Bradford's face, the smug half-smile that said that the argument was over—at least as far as he was concerned—was so familiar to Gold that he might as well have seen it just yesterday. The expression wiped away the years, and Gold felt a sudden wave of sorrow, as if he were looking at his old friend in his Academy days, full of pride and optimism and the sense that all the doors in the universe were open to him, and he had only to choose which one to pass through first.

"Come on, Gus. Be a *mensch* for once. Release your hostages and work this out the right way."

Bradford's answer was slow in coming, as if he had to think it over, even though, in fact, it could have been foreordained. *"Sorry, David,"* he said at last. *"No surrender."*

Gold pounded a fist on his desk. "Dammit, man, they're going to kill you! They don't negotiate with terrorists, and they're going to wipe out the base—including Deborah and Ben!"

"Their deaths will be on Aulyffke's head, not mine."

"What the hell difference does it make *whose* head it's on? They'll still be dead—just because they had the fool notion that visiting you was a *good* idea. Does Deborah deserve to die because she just wanted you to meet your grandson? Does Ben deserve to have his entire *life* taken away from him because you need to prove a point?"

Bradford said nothing. Just the fact that he had managed to shut Gus up emboldened Gold.

"I'm not asking you to surrender a damn thing, Gus. I just want don't want to see a Federation dignitary and two people whom you supposedly love die, just so you can win one more argument."

"Don't you dare try to tell me that I don't love my daughter, David. Don't you dare!"

"Then prove it. Don't murder them needlessly."

"You don't understand, I have to show—"

Gold leaned forward. "Oh, I understand just fine, Gus. I know how your mind works. You go out in a blaze of glory, take innocents with you, and that'll prove you right. But it won't help your cause a single bit. You want the Federation out of Kursican. That's fine—but if you let Uree die with you, the Federation will be all over Kursican like matzoh balls in chicken soup. If you let them go, though, Uree can report back just what happened here today."

"So can you."

"Think about what I'd say if you let them die, Gus."

The pause that followed seemed to last for hours.

Then, suddenly, Bradford cut off the connection.

"Dammit!" Gold tapped his combadge. "Ina, reestablish communications!"

"They're not responding, sir."

"Feliciano, any luck?"

"*No, sir, but—hold on.*" After a pause, he went on. "*Somebody beaming onto the* da Vinci *from the station, sir. Three figures—bioreadings are one Deltan and two humans.*"

Gold breathed a sigh of relief.

CHAPTER
11

"*Commander Gomez,*" Hawkins's voice came over her combadge. He sounded nervous. "*Some of the prisoners are getting out of the line. They're forming—well, I guess you'd call it a mob. And they're eyeing my phaser.*"

"*Now do you believe me, Commander?*" Corsi asked.

"I didn't disbelieve you," Sonya replied. "But we have our orders. Stand your ground, Mr. Hawkins."

A thousand prisoners. Sixteen Starfleet personnel. One didn't have to be an engineer to know the math was unfavorable.

Her combadge chirped again, followed by Captain Gold's voice. "*I'm pulling your team out, Gomez,*" he said. "*Stand by for transport.*"

"But, sir—there are still injured prisoners awaiting treatment. And the Kursicans aren't here yet."

"*Their ship is on the way,*" Gold said. "*They'll be there in twenty minutes or so.*"

"They may have an unpleasant reception when they get here."

"That's their problem, Commander. Not yours."

"Yes, sir. What about Bradford and the hostages?"

"We have Ambassador Uree and the other two hostages safe on board."

Sonya Gomez smiled for the first time since they'd arrived in the Kursican system. "I'm glad to hear that, sir. And Bradford?"

A hesitation. *"Gus and his followers were wiped out by Kursican authorities ten minutes ago."*

The smile fell. "Captain—I'm so sorry, I—"

"Save it. Get back up here."

"Yes, sir."

Once a course had been set and warp speed achieved out of the Kursican system, Gold joined the away team in the mess hall. None of them had eaten anything since their trip to the Plat, and they were starving. For his part, he was just glad they'd all come out unhurt. He had lost enough for one day.

He had visited Ambassador Uree, then been reunited with his goddaughter, though it was something less than a happy reunion. To Gold's surprise, Deborah's primary emotion wasn't sadness or anger at her father's death—it was pity. Whether for Gus, for the Kursicans, or both, Gold couldn't say.

"As far as I'm concerned," Domenica Corsi said between mouthfuls, "they should be banned from the Federation forever."

"I'm inclined to agree," Sonya said. She took a sip of Earl Grey. "They have a long way to go in terms of being civilized."

"But maybe the Federation's influence on them would be a good one, Sonnie," Kieran pointed out. "You're right, they have a long way to go. But if we just turn our backs on them, what motivation do they have to change?"

"Who cares if they do?" Sonya shot back, setting her teacup down on the table with a clatter. She wiped a lock of hair back from her forehead and looked around the table. "I'm sorry, Kieran. All of you, really. This hasn't been a good day for me."

"We noticed," Corsi said, hiding her smile by touching her lips with a napkin.

"I don't even like zoos," Sonya explained. "And as for prisons? I hoped never to have to visit one in my life. All those people, penned like animals—I don't care what they did. There must be a better way to deal with them."

"What about you, Captain Gold?" Duffy asked. "What do you think?"

Gold hesitated a moment before speaking. "I just talked with Ambassador Uree. He is going to strongly recommend that the Federation deny their application," he said. "But they'll probably reconsider it at some point in the not-too-distant future. That's why they're politicians and I'm just a starship captain—they can overlook savagery when it's expedient to do so. I'm just not built that way. Gus Bradford was wrong, and he was a stubborn damn fool, and if he brought on his own death, then so be it." He stopped then, rage and sorrow fighting for primacy in his heart, and swallowed once.

"Anyway," he continued. "We're well away from there now. God willing, we'll never go back. Let's talk about something else."

CAVEAT EMPTOR

Ian Edginton & Mike Collins

CHAPTER
1

Forg held his breath and listened intently, straining to detect even the slightest sound.

There was nothing.

A trickle of cold sweat snaked its way down the back of his neck, quickly prompting him to bite his lip, stifling a sudden squeak of terror. Under normal circumstances, the halls of a Ferengi Merchantman positively buzzed with the chatter of conspiracies and intrigue and of deals being struck. But now there wasn't even the reassuringly sensual chink of gold-pressed latinum.

It was . . . unnatural.

Forg prided himself on having the kind of lobes that could detect the unique sound of a strip of latinum being dropped thirty meters away. In fact, during his apprenticeship back in the Commercial and Mercantile Institute of Ferenginar, he could correctly identify seventy-five different forms of currency just from the way they hit the ground. His father had been so impressed that he'd bought him an Institute Commendation, to be deducted against his future earnings, of course.

Forg nibbled uncomfortably at his lip. The discomfort was nothing compared to the growing fear in his stomach. It was either that or the spore pie he'd eaten after he'd finished his shift six hours ago.

Six hours, had it been only that long?

He reached a junction and hesitated. Flattening himself against the wall, he peered tentatively around the corner. The corridor beyond was deserted. He allowed himself the luxury of exhaling. At the far end lay the escape pods. If he could just keep his nerve for a little while longer, he would be free of this nightmare. Tiptoeing as gingerly as he dared, he cast quick glances at the doorways on either side, expecting them to suddenly hiss open at any second and see one of *them* standing there.

Forg froze. There was something on the floor just ahead. He recognized it as a strip of latinum. What's more, it was still in its mint wraps. And it wasn't alone. There were others, lots of them. So many, in fact, he could buy this ship a hundred times over and still have enough change to keep him hip-deep in Dabo girls for life. Forg felt the familiar tingling sensation of greed washing over him.

He followed the glittering trail to the bank of escape pods. A green light winked on the control console above one of the hatches. A pod had been launched. Someone else had escaped.

Down at his feet, a gray security crate lay on its

side, spilling latinum. Like the rest they were all still in their wraps, as shiny and pristine as the day they were minted. He recognized the family crest stamped on the wraps. This wasn't just anyone's personal hoard. It belonged to the ship's owner, DaiMon Phug.

Forg's momentary glee soon faded as he wondered what it was that could force Phug to abandon his fortune barely a meter away from freedom? Whatever it was, it wasn't there now and as such was Phug's loss. Forg balanced his fear against his avarice and found they came out pretty even. He decided to go with the latter; after all wasn't it the Sixty-Second Rule of Acquisition that stated, "The riskier the road, the greater the profit"?

Besides, he had a plan.

He popped the hatch of the nearest pod and began loading the latinum inside. Initially, he assured himself, he was going to take only the strips that were within arm's length. There was no need to take foolish risks.

But . . .

To abandon those strips only a few steps away seemed foolish, not to mention wasteful. So he took the steps, then some more, and even more still, each time scuttling back to hurl another armful into the pod, mentally tallying up the worth of each load.

A matching pair of latinum lobe buffers and fang sharpeners. A complete lifetime's wardrobe of the finest Tholian silk (including underwear). An estate in the Colloid marshes. A brand-new, not reconditioned, trading schooner with its own captain's yacht. A moon—maybe two.

Plus, of course, a substantial donation to the Prophets of the Divine Treasury—ensuring his name was recited in the Annual Tally so that he might be looked upon favorably by the Blessed Exchequer and the Celestial Auctioneers. Forg wasn't usually so diligent in his spiritual devotions, but it never hurt to hedge your bets.

Somewhere among his fantasies of prospective underwear, real estate, and a comfortable afterlife, Forg failed to hear the hiss that he'd so previously dreaded. However, his terror returned with a vengeance as he waddled down the corridor laden with booty only to be confronted by a short, dark stranger. The tumbling latinum bruised two of his toes but fear had stolen Forg's voice.

The figure was dressed in a floor-length hooded robe improvised from black cargo sheeting. In his hand, a staff as tall as the figure himself was cut from a section of conduit piping. The figure slowly lifted his head to face him. Forg's eyes widened in recognition.

"Zin?" he finally croaked, incredulous.

No, not anymore, Forg realized. He began to slowly back away, managing only a few agonizing steps before the ominous rustle of more robes behind him rooted him to the spot.

"Please," he whispered, "don't." But his plea fell on large, deaf ears.

He saw Zin's dead eyes.

He saw the staff.

After that . . . nothing.

CHAPTER
2

The tiny Klingon paced furiously along the top of Captain David Gold's desk, neatly skirting a cinnamon bagel before resting his spiked boot defiantly on the lip of a china saucer.

"No, no, *no!*" he snarled. The frustration was evident in his contorted little face. "Your enunciation is a disgrace. Do you even know what a syllable is?"

Gold set down his coffee cup. He contemplated replying but thought better of it. The small holographic Klingon was clearly on a roll.

"And as for your pronunciation! Pfagh!" he spat with undisguised venom. "You sound like a toothless old man too long in his cups!"

"I understand," Gold replied with bemusement bordering on irritation.

"In Klingon!" bellowed the warrior, who looked to Gold as if he were about to have an aneurysm any second.

"*jIyajchu,*" Gold answered, attempting to correctly pronounce the uniquely hacking, phlegmy sound that punctuated most Klingon grammar. The warrior gave a sharp snort of approval just as the door chime to Gold's quarters sounded.

"Saved by the bell," he muttered. "Come."

Commander Sonya Gomez, the *da Vinci*'s first officer entered, breaking into a broad beaming grin when she saw the miniature Klingon glowering up at Gold.

"Good morning, Captain. I hope that I'm not interrupting?"

"Interrupt away," he said, glancing over at the small, antique silver traveling clock. A captain's timepiece from the Napoleonic Wars, it had been a gift from his wife, Rachel, on their twenty-fifth wedding anniversary. "I'm just about finished here."

"But I am not!" the warrior bellowed. "We are done when I say so!"

"Like hell. End program."

The fuming Klingon dissipated into a swirling cluster of light particles, returning to the small oval holo-emitter on Gold's desk. A single red light winked like an angry red eye, signifying that the program had been shut down.

"Now, if I could have done that to certain teachers at the Academy, I'd have been the most popular person in my year."

Gomez smiled. "Every student's fantasy. I didn't know you were interested in learning Klingon."

"I'm not—exactly." Gold indicated the holo-emitter. "This was a gift from my granddaughter, Esther—you remember, Daniel's youngest? Her new beau is a Klingon politician, and she insists I bone up on the rudiments of the language so I can address him correctly. I think she's reprogrammed it herself to reflect a more realistic Klingon temperament. She's a tinkerer. Wants to be an engineer . . . this week at least. She sent it to me a month ago, but I didn't really start using it until—" He hesitated.

"Kursican?" Gomez prompted.

Gold heaved a heavy sigh. "Let's just say that after what happened with Gus Bradford on Kursican, I've become a lot more conscious of family." Brightening a bit, he went on: "In any event, we're all supposed to be having dinner on my next shore leave. Poor Rachel's going frantic trying to find a recipe for a kosher blood pie."

Remembering the background of one of her old crewmates on the *Enterprise*, Gomez said, "Tell her to get in touch with Sergey and Helena Rozhenko. Sergey is retired Starfleet—I think they live in Minsk. They raised Ambassador Worf."

Standing up, Gold smiled. "Thank you, Commander, I'll be sure to recommend that." He offered Gomez the door. "Shall we?"

They walked in the direction of the bridge, Gomez taking her place beside her captain, quickening her pace to match his.

Gold enjoyed these brief moments of informality. There was no real reason for Gomez to escort her CO to the bridge at the start of their duty shift save for they fact they both enjoyed the small talk and each other's company. It was difficult working away from family for such long stretches. Unlike other starships, the size of the *da Vinci* and the often hazardous nature of its mission meant she was not designed or equipped to carry both crew and their families. Gold had been concerned that Gomez would curtail the practice once she and Kieran Duffy, the *da Vinci*'s second officer, had rekindled their romance, but that had not been the case.

"Dating a Klingon," Gomez said with a small smile. "That can be tricky."

"I know," said Gold. "But Esther's no slouch. Apparently they've been inseparable since they met—you couldn't stick a pin between them. I think it's a case of an irresistible force meeting an immovable object."

"Does the immovable object have a name?" enquired Gomez.

"Khor, son of Lantar—of the House of Gorkon."

"Wow," Gomez said. Gorkon was the chancellor who brokered the first of the Khitomer Accords with the Federation after the destruction of Praxis eighty years earlier.

"He was one of the youngest captains to command a fleet during the war. Last month, he was appointed to Chancellor Martok's staff."

"A highflyer in every sense of the word. How did Esther snag him?" asked Gomez. "Not that she isn't capable," she added quickly.

Gold sighed in that indulgent, paternal way that Esther always made fun of.

"She got into an argument with him in a bar."

Gomez winced. "A bar?"

Gold nodded. "I know. Don't ask. I didn't. It's

easier on the nerves that way. Since finishing college, she's been backpacking around the galaxy while she tries to figure out what she wants to do with her life. Seems she crossed paths with Khor and his colleagues while they were out on a binge. They saw her and started going on about human history. We had no truly great deeds or battles worthy of song and saga, the usual nonsense." Gold shook his head, smiling. "So my Esther—no taller than a Ferengi, but with a temper that would give a Gorn a hard time—calls them out and informs them in language that would make a Nausicaan blush that they are mistaken."

"So what happened?" asked Gomez as they entered the turbolift. "Bridge," she added, and the turbolift sped upward.

Gold paused, his face suddenly solemn. "She told them, in great detail, about the Romans' siege of Masada, of the thousand Jewish partisans—men, women, and children—who sacrificed themselves rather than return to a life of slavery and oppression." He brightened. "She must've made an impression, because Khor apologized and escorted her to where she was staying. The next day he invited her to an opera recital and they haven't been apart since."

The doors to the turbolift opened and the captain and first officer entered the bridge. Lieutenant McAllan half turned and said, "Captain on the bridge."

"Knock it off, McAllan," Gold said. He generally ran a comparatively informal bridge, and never insisted on the particular protocol that required bellowing his entrance like some kind of—well, Roman emperor. But McAllan, the *da Vinci*'s tactical officer, kept insisting, no doubt encouraged by the ship's chief of security, the ever-spit-and-polish Domenica Corsi. "Status?"

"We were just going to call you, actually, sir," McAllan said. "We're picking up an automated transmission from an unidentified vessel sixty thousand kilometers off our starboard bow. Based on the initial readings, it's an escape pod."

From the ops console in front of the captain's chair, Lieutenant Ina Mar said, "Captain, they've picked up on our scans. They're firing maneuvering thrusters"—her eyes widened—"in the opposite direction."

"They're trying to outrun us?" Gomez asked.

"This I have to see," added Gold. "On screen."

The vast panoramic expanse of a starfield on the forward viewer was replaced by a less panoramic expanse, with something that looked like a pale orange beetle at its center. It was a ship, oval in shape, covered in overlapping bands of riveted metal. Its underside was flat and smooth with a pair of forward-facing wings sweeping from halfway along its sides, tapering down to narrow points at the front. At the rear, a cluster of exhaust vents glowed white as they attempted to propel the tiny craft away from the *da Vinci*.

"Getting its registry now, sir," McAllan said. "It's a Ferengi lifepod."

"I'll be damned," said Gold. "Hail them, McAllan. Let's see what they're up to."

"Yes, sir." McAllan opened a channel. "This is

the *U.S.S. da Vinci* to Ferengi pod, please acknowledge."

There was no reply.

Gold nodded at the screen. "Keep knocking,
McAllan."

"I repeat, this is the *U.S.S. da Vinci* to Ferengi
pod, please respo—"

"Go away!" The reply was on audio only but
there was no mistaking the vehemence in the tone.

"I'd say that qualifies as a response," Gold muttered.

Gomez moved to the tactical station next to
McAllan, but spoke to the ship's conn officer.
"Ensign Wong, get us into tractor-beam range."

"Aye, sir," replied Songmin Wong.

"Ferengi pod," Gomez said, "please disengage
your thrusters and prepare to be taken under tow."

*"Are you deaf, human? I am perfectly fine and in
no need of assistance. Now, withdraw immediately!"*

Ina turned around. "Sensors indicate no
Class-M planets nor other ships within the pod's
range. If we don't bring him in, no one will."

Gomez nodded. "Ferengi pod, under the articles
of interstellar law, we are legally obliged to render
aid and assistance to any ship in distress. By its
very nature, your escape pod qualifies as just that.
Furthermore, we are your only chance for rescue."

"You cannot . . ." was the spluttering reply.

Gomez motioned to McAllan to cut the link.

"In tractor-beam range now," Wong reported.

"Reel him in, Mr. McAllan," she said.

Gold nodded approvingly, then tapped his combadge. "Transporter room. Feliciano, lock onto the

pilot of that pod and beam him directly to sickbay on my mark."

"Yes, sir."

Gomez said, "With your permission, sir, I'll greet our guest."

"Granted. Bridge to sickbay—Dr. Lense, prepare to accept an agitated, possibly disturbed Ferengi patient."

"We'll be waiting," said the ship's chief medical officer.

As the turbolift swallowed Gomez back up, Gold made one final call, to the ship's second officer. "Duffy, as soon as that pod's secure in the hangar, go over it with a fine-tooth comb."

"On my way, sir."

CHAPTER
3

"Eeeeeee!!!"

The Ferengi's continued squealing set Dr. Elizabeth Lense's teeth on edge and shredded what remained of her patience. She was all for pastoral care, but right now all she wanted to do was stuff a sock in her whining patient's mouth.

The Ferengi was dressed head to foot in black and purple velvet. The high collar and cuffs of his tailcoat were trimmed with elegant silver embroidery, the buttonholes and elaborate detailing picked out in gold thread. He also hadn't stopped screaming since Chief Feliciano's transporter beam deposited him on a biobed.

"What are you complaining about? I haven't even touched you," she said, lowering the medical tricorder.

"And you're not going to, at least until you've taken your clothes off!"

"Sorry," Lense said with a sigh, "never on a first date."

"Is there a problem?" Gomez asked, entering the room, flanked by Lt. Commander Corsi and one of the security guards, Andrea Lipinski.

"More clothed females!" exclaimed the Ferengi. "This is an obscenity! First you seize my ship against my express wishes. Then you proceed to abduct me and subject me to this probing and inquisition, and now you surround me with clothed females!"

"I thought the new Grand Nagus had lifted the restrictions against Ferengi women," Gomez said.

The Ferengi sneered. "Just because the nagus-hood was granted to an idiot who has spent too much time among humans such as yourselves doesn't mean we have all turned our back on tradi-tional values. I demand to speak to a male in charge!"

"I've had enough of this," Lense said. "Computer, activate Emergency Medical Hologram."

A dark-skinned, pleasant-faced figure material-ized in the center of the room. "Good afternoon, Doctor," the holographic physician, whom Lense had nicknamed "Emmett," said.

Lense handed Emmett her tricorder. "This patient requires a physical exam. If you'll excuse me, Commander," she added to Gomez, then went into her office.

Emmett looked befuddled only for a moment, then started his examination. The Ferengi looked dubious, but was apparently satisfied that this was a male, even if he was a hologram, and didn't balk at the exam.

Gomez sighed. "I apologize for any distress, but

it *is* part of Starfleet's business to render aid and protection to the weak and the vulnerable. A lone escape craft adrift in deep space strikes me as being just that."

"I knew what I was doing, female," the Ferengi said derisively. "There are dozens of worlds in the system where I could have made planetfall."

"According to our sensors, none of the worlds in this system can sustain humanoid life."

"Bah," the Ferengi said, slumping his shoulders.

Emmett said, "If you could please sit still, Mr.—?"

"My name is Phug—DaiMon Phug."

Gomez frowned. The title of DaiMon was given only to ship captains in the Ferengi Alliance. "DaiMon Phug, what happened to your ship?" she asked. "Should we be searching for other life-pods?"

"No . . . there's no need . . . there aren't any others. They're all dead. When we lost containment . . . the warp field collapsed. There was scarcely time to reach the escape pods. I almost didn't make it."

"I'm sorry for the loss of your crew."

"My crew? Pah! If they'd been up to snuff this never would have happened! I always knew it was a mistake signing on a chief engineer who couldn't count to twenty without taking his shoes off. The Ferengi education system isn't what it once was, you know."

"If you'll permit the doctor to finish his examination, I'll assign you quarters. We can discuss where you wish to be set down later. Would you like me to notify the Alliance that we've picked you up?"

"*No!* I will see to it, thank you."

"You're welcome." To the hologram, she said, "Carry on, Emmett."

"Of course, Commander."

Gomez and Corsi left, Corsi nodding to Lipinski, indicating that she was to stay and keep an eye on the Ferengi.

As soon as the doors closed behind them, Corsi said, "Commander, you know he's lying, don't you?"

Nodding, Gomez said, "Through his pointy little teeth." She tapped her combadge. "Gomez to Duffy."

"Go ahead, Sonnie."

Gomez shook her head. Part of her found it endearing when Duffy called her that, but it wasn't entirely appropriate when they were both on duty. "Kieran, let me know as soon as you're done going over the pod. Our guest says he barely escaped a containment breach. I want that verified."

"On it, but I'm not seeing any indications that this was near any kind of breach. Initial scan doesn't show any of the usual particulate traces."

"No surprise there," Corsi muttered.

"Keep me posted, Kieran. Gomez out."

CHAPTER
4

It was raining on Ferenginar.

In fact, it always rained on Ferenginar—even during the alleged dry season when it simply rained less.

Several xeno-anthropologists posited the radical theory that this consistently inclement weather was actually the cornerstone of the Ferengi culture. This was reflected in the Ferengi language itself, which had no less than one hundred and seventy-eight words for "rain"—and no word for "crisp." With little else to do but huddle in their burrows while the deluge persisted, the early Ferengi would pass the long hours trying to work out ways of keeping warm, dry, and comfortable. They eventually came to the conclusion that the only practical solution to their problem primarily revolved around the acquisition of huge amounts of cash. It was the great thinker Gint (who later went on to become Ferenginar's first Grand Nagus) who stated, "Money can't buy you love but it can buy you an umbrella."

It was, some claimed, from this simple desire that the entire Ferengi social, political, and religious structure evolved to create the foremost trading race in known space. Ironically it also led, millennia later, to the creation of the only desert on Ferenginar.

The Nimbi Massif was a vast rift valley terraformed into an arid, bone-dry expanse, its climate maintained by a series of colossal dehumidifiers. This change of environment enabled the valley to be lined with an array of parabolic baffles, transforming the entire geographic feature into a gigantic transceiver dish—a huge ear turned toward the sky. Via this dish, the Ferengi government could eavesdrop on interstellar communications, tracking the movements of stocks, shares, currency fluctuations, and investments across several sectors. Not to mention more politically sensitive data that had a price all its own.

Consequently, the Nimbi Array was staffed around the clock by a legion of eager listeners, all sifting, extrapolating, and interpreting the incoming material, aurally panning for nuggets of fiscal data from the great rivers of interstellar chatter.

Interpolator Brusk was one such listener. He was also the first to encounter the heretic . . . but he wouldn't be the last.

Brusk had devoted almost six months to monitoring communications from Breen space. The Breen economy had been in turmoil ever since the fall of the Dominion and the reparations imposed by the Federation/Klingon/Romulan alliance, prompting them to consider selling the secrets behind their formidable technology. At one point during the war, the Breen energy-dissipating weapons almost brought the Alliance to its knees. Sensing that blood was in the water and a considerable return could be had, Brusk sat and waited and listened.

Now his dedication was looking to pay off. The Breen government had gone into session to decide which course of action to take. Brusk knew that selling was their only option and he had requested a negotiating team to remain on standby, ready to approach the Breen with a deal within hours of their decision. Of course, in keeping with the great Ferengi tradition of shameless nepotism, the team included his two brothers and several nephews.

Tugging at his right lobe with nervous excitement, Brusk leaned closer to his computer console, intently watching the screen as the internal communications traffic from within Breen space scrolled in front of him, the universal translator changing the complex Breen word forms into legible text. The session would finish any time now and the minutes of the meeting downloaded to their central files . . . via a brief detour to Ferenginar.

Suddenly, the unfurling text vanished from the screen, replaced by a wash of static and white noise. Brusk moaned in disbelief. He tapped frantically at the keypad, desperately attempting to reboot the system, but to no avail. Brusk stood and peered over the partition at the Ferengi at the next work station. Rhut specialized in Klingon commodities, mostly Kohlar beast bellies and bloodwine, but he was also pretty handy with computers. He'd charge Brusk through the nose to fix his machine but with the state of play so critical it was worth the outlay.

Brusk put on his best poker face, ready to haggle. "Rhut, my console's just crashed. I . . . ."

Rhut didn't pay him any attention. He was too busy concentrating on the screen in front of him, his fingers dancing urgently over the keyboard.

"So? Join the club," he snapped. "But you better have backed up your files because it looks like the entire system's gone down."

Brusk glanced out over the hangar-like expanse of the work floor. Hundreds of his fellow interpolators had abandoned their work stations and were gathered in nervous huddles. He could taste the panic in the air.

This was bad. This was very bad.

Then Rhut announced, "It's back up!"

The static had cleared, but the screen was now blank. As Brusk watched, a face began to resolve out of the gray nothingness. All the other Ferengi were as equally fixed to their screens. Whatever was happening, it was cutting in on *all* bandwidths and frequencies. The vast expanse of the Nimbi Array was receiving just one signal to the exclusion of all else.

A Ferengi face filled the screen, but it wasn't like any Ferengi Brusk had ever seen. The head was longer than normal, with fine, high cheekbones and an elegant, aquiline nose. The eyes were wide and compassionate. Even the lobes seemed to be more sculpted and swept back.

The face was . . . beautiful. Brusk found it unsettling, but there was worse to come.

The face smiled, showing two rows of white, even teeth. Brusk shuddered.

"Peace, joy and contentment to you all, my brothers and sisters . . . I am Milia. I am coming home."

Brusk screamed . . .

. . . along with every other Ferengi in the room.

CHAPTER
5

Sonya Gomez leaned against the wall of the turbolift, her arms crossed. She gently tapped the padd in her left hand against her chin.

Duffy had been the very model of efficiency, and had produced a detailed report, with full spectrographic analysis of Phug's lifepod. Gomez had then reviewed the system diagnostics and had reluctantly agreed with the findings. It was Gomez's task as first officer to present the results and conclusions to her captain. Unfortunately, the answers Duffy had obtained only posed more questions.

She sighed. *Why did it have to be a Ferengi?*

Gomez had to admit that her opinions of the trader race were inevitably colored by her experiences aboard the *Enterprise*. About a year before she signed on to the Federation's flagship as an engineer, Captain Picard had the first visual contact with the Ferengi. Since then, the ship had been involved in many encounters with the race, and Gomez, who, working in engineering, was often involved in cleaning up the mess left by the latest Ferengi scheme against the crew, had developed an unhealthy distrust of the race. That distrust was fostered by the fact that the Ferengi were the ones who opened the first trade relations with the Dominion. Gomez had always wondered in the back of her head whether or not the war would have turned out the way it did if it had been the Federation that made first contact instead of the Ferengi.

Intellectually, she knew that her distrustful attitude was at odds with Starfleet's all-embracing philosophy. She needed to get past it—especially today, dealing with Phug and his pod.

The turbolift eased to a halt, the doors slid open onto the bridge. Duffy was at the conn, and he smiled at her. "Ready to give the captain the bad news?" he asked, getting up from the command chair.

She nodded, and they both went into the ready room.

"Tell me you have good news, Gomez," Gold said.

"I'm afraid not, sir. There's no evidence of any damage at all. None of the particulate traces you'd expect from a warp core breach, minimal hull scarring, none of which matches what you'd get from an antimatter explosion, no radioactivity beyond the usual background radiation of space. And, before you ask, there's no sign of distress from any kind of energy weapon—he wasn't running from a firefight, either."

"Or," Duffy added, "if he was, he did it without getting hit once, which is pretty unlikely in a pod with only type-two maneuvering thrusters."

Gold blew out a breath. "He was running from *something*. What would spook a Ferengi DaiMon that much?"

"Someone's found a way of replicating latinum?" Duffy joked.

Indicating the padd's screen, Gomez said, "One bit of good news—we know the course he took."

"Good," Gold said. "Any information about Phug or his ship?"

Gomez shook her head. "No, there wasn't anything useful in the pod's computer. I can't imagine a Ferengi would put anything like that in an escape pod's databank where anyone could access it without paying for the privilege."

"Good point."

Duffy rubbed his chin. "Might be worth putting a call in to Deep Space 9. See if our old pal Nog knows anything about Phug."

Gomez remembered that Lieutenant Nog—the first Ferengi to ever join Starfleet and the chief operations officer of DS9—had worked with the *da Vinci* crew at Empok Nor a while back. Gomez herself hadn't been around for that, busy as she was with a mission to Sarindar, but she did know one thing: Nog was the son of the new Grand Nagus, Rom. Rom himself was a former engineer on DS9—that was the time spent among humans that Phug had found so distasteful—and the architect of the brilliant self-replicating minefield that had held the Dominion in check for precious, valuable months while the Federation amassed its forces.

"Couldn't hurt," Gold said with a nod. "Have McAllan get in touch with Nog and have Wong backtrack Phug's course. My curiosity's been piqued now."

"Mine, too," Gomez said. "It's not like Phug himself has been forthcoming."

Within ten minutes, Wong had set a course back along the pod's route and McAllan had sent a message to Deep Space 9.

Within fifteen minutes, the *da Vinci* was rocked by a gravity wave of some kind. "All stop!" Gomez said. "Captain Gold to the bridge."

"Answering all stop," Wong said.

"What the hell was that?" Gold said as he entered the bridge.

"Some kind of gravity wave," Duffy said from an aft engineering station. "Something's generating a massive field, but we're not picking up anything except normal space."

"Damage report," Gomez said to McAllan as she vacated the command chair for Gold.

McAllan checked his status board. "No significant damage. A few bumps and bruises."

"We're picking something up now," Duffy said. "Wow."

Gomez joined Duffy at the console. "Could you be a little more specific?"

"Not really," Duffy said. "Take a look."

She looked at his console, and saw an amazing sight. "Wow," she said. "Put it on the main viewer, Kieran."

Everyone turned to the viewscreen, which now displayed a Ferengi Merchantman. A floating commerce vessel, it was a virtual city in space. Never a race to allow aesthetics to get in the way of practicalities, they had designed the Merchantman as an enormous version of their regular Ferengi vessels, but absurdly large—five decks where there was one on the original. It gleamed a tarnished gold, somehow brassy in the blackness of space. It was at once ludicrous and threatening.

Gold was actually open-mouthed. "How the *hell* did that thing appear out of nowhere?"

"I don't know, sir," Duffy said, "but it didn't register on the sensors until we came within fifty thousand kilometers of it."

"Try to hail them, McAllan," Gold said.

"Aye, sir."

Moving to stand next to the operations console, Gomez asked the Bajoran woman seated there, "Mar, what can you tell me about the ship?"

"Registry lists it as the Ferengi Merchantman *Debenture of Triple-Lined Latinum*," Ina Mar said.

"That's a mouthful," Wong muttered with a smile.

Ina continued: "Three kilometers in diameter, crew capacity of thirty thousand, though I can't get any definitive lifesigns right now. According to the database, it's owned and operated by DaiMon Phug."

Duffy grinned. "We have a winner."

Gold turned to McAllan. "Where's Phug now?"

"Emmett gave him a physical—he checked out

fine. Corsi stuck him in the mess hall with two guards on him."

Frowning, Gold repeated, "*Emmett* gave him a physical?"

"The DaiMon had a problem being examined by a '*fee*-male,'" Gomez said, impersonating the way Phug had sneered the word in sickbay.

Gold grumbled something, then said, "Put a call through to him. And keep trying to raise that monster out there."

Phug's high-pitched whine of a voice came on a moment later. "*I demand an explanation for this disruption of my well-being!*"

"This is Captain Gold. We were retracing your pod's route. It took us right to your ship."

"*You found my ship?*"

Gomez shot a glance at Gold. Phug had been indignant—now he was out-and-out scared.

"*Get . . . us . . . out . . . of . . . here . . . now!*"

Before Gold could reply, the ship shook again. "Report!" the captain bellowed.

"We've been caught in a tractor beam," Duffy said.

"Break us loose," Gold said to Wong.

Wong tried to activate the impulse engines, but the *da Vinci* didn't move. "We can't break free, Captain."

"*You fools!*" came Phug's voice—at once smug and scared. "*You've doomed us all!*"

CHAPTER
6

Phug was not happy about being escorted to the *da Vinci* bridge—especially not by two clothed females. What he wanted was to be taken to his escape pod so he could use it to escape again. Maybe this time he'd find a planet where he could lie low for a bit and reestablish himself, rather than a Starfleet ship that insisted on bringing him back to the very thing he was trying to escape from. He was sure they were lying about there being no habitable planets in the system. You couldn't trust humans. . . .

Instead, the human female Corsi and her subordinate took him to the bridge, where the human DaiMon—*what are they called*, he thought, *"kaptans"?*—sat waiting for him. Also present were a bunch of other humans—including, to his disgust, more clothed females—as well as a Bajoran and, surprisingly, a single Bynar. *I thought those computer-lovers all came in pairs.* Still, at least the Bynar was almost normal-looking, though he did, of course, have the same hideously stunted ears as the others.

"DaiMon Phug, I'm Captain Gold. I wish I could say it's a pleasure to meet you, but considering that your ship is holding mine in a tractor beam right now—"

"I accept no responsibility, Captain!" Phug cried. "I never asked you to come back to the *Debenture*."

"In fact, you told us the *Debenture* had exploded. Mind telling us why you *really* left?"

Phug said nothing. He saw no reason to just *give* information to this human, and it's not like someone from Starfleet would ever pay for it. So he remained silent.

"All right, let's start smaller—how come we didn't see the *Debenture* before it was too late?"

Again, Phug stood his ground—until the female Corsi put her hand to her phaser. Gold might have been a typical Starfleet weakling with no lobes for business, but Phug recognized in Corsi the type who liked to extort by the barrel of a phaser. *This*, he thought sourly, *is what happens when you clothe females. They get delusions of Klingonhood. . . .*

"Multiple cloaks," he said. "Some Klingon, some Romulan. The Merchantman is so vast that it would overload a single device. There is a cloak array around the perimeter; they allow us to enter a trading area before the local customer base is aware of us."

Corsi smiled. "The One Hundred and Ninety-Fourth Rule of Acquisition: 'It's always good business to know about your customers before they walk in your door.' You find out what they have the most need of and then magically appear to provide it."

Phug regarded the female with revulsion. To hear the Rules coming from a female mouth—it was despicable. He quickly turned his gaze back to the captain.

The female named Gomez was standing next to Gold. "You run *several* cloaks—that's got to require a huge amount of power."

Phug shrugged. "We acquire the technology we need to run the systems. We're traders, after all."

Gold cut him off. "As interesting as this is—and at some point there are questions you'll have to answer about how exactly you acquired this cloaking technology—we need more information from you. Can you override that tractor beam?"

Phug was about to ask why he should, when it occurred to him that he was as trapped as they were. The *da Vinci* would never break free of the *Debenture*'s tractor beam. So it was in his own interests to acquiesce. He went to the tactical station and tapped in a code sequence, ignoring the doleful look the human male at that station gave him. "There. That will free your ship. It isn't a threatening device; its purpose is to maintain the proximity of ships of visiting customers. When you have purchased goods, there is a release code issued. I believe you have a similar tradition on your planet: validated parking."

Corsi looked incredulous. "You trap your customers?"

Phug was offended. This female quoted the Rules, yet had no comprehension of them. "No—how can you imply that? We just want you to buy goods, then you're free to go."

"So by transmitting this code, the *Debenture* will assume we've conducted a transaction and then free us?" asked Gold.

Phug nodded, glad that the male, at least, understood business matters. "You must destroy this information immediately—if the Commerce Authority found I'd revealed this code, I could lose my credit rating."

Gold was about to reply when the ship lurched, throwing Phug to the floor.

"Report!" Gold bellowed, having managed somehow to stay in his chair.

"The tractor beam disengaged, sir," the human at tactical said, "but some kind of energy beam came from the *Debenture*. Now *it's* trapped us."

The Bynar spoke from one of the aft consoles. "Captain, something is attempting to take control of our computer systems!"

Gold looked at Phug questioningly.

"What?" Phug asked defensively. "I'm as surprised by this as you are!"

Gomez walked up to the Bynar. "Can you stop it, Soloman?"

"I'm attempting to do so now." The Bynar—who, to Phug's surprise, had a name rather than a numerical designation; Phug filed that fact away for potential future use, assuming he lived long enough—then let loose with a stream of high-pitched droning. "It's some kind of intelligent worm—it's very sophisticated. I will need to focus."

"Go to it," Gomez said, backing away.

Soloman chirped that droning some more. Phug put his hands to his ears. "Must he make that horrid noise here?"

"Suffer," Corsi said, again putting her hand to her phaser.

Then the droning mercifully stopped. "Commander Gomez," Soloman said, "I can only hold off this invasive program for a limited time. It needs to be stopped at the source." Then the droning started again, stopped. "I must be vigilant here, or the *da Vinci* systems will be compromised."

Gomez looked at Gold. "We'll have to send an away team over there."

"Put it together, Gomez." Gold turned to Phug. "We'll need your help, Phug."

Phug looked around the bridge, realizing there was no escape from this. Why did these Starfleet types have to be so eager and earnest? Why couldn't they have let him go, left him to float in his pod until he'd found a young, fresh world where he could introduce the natives to the holy joys of commerce, could amass a fiscal empire, make himself a new life, and forget about this debacle? But no—these tiresome humans dragged him back to face . . . he couldn't even think the words.

"I shall aid you . . . but on the strict understanding that I *will not* set foot on that ship. I will provide you with specifications and routes to disable the computer systems . . . and when you are done I wish to leave here and never return!"

"Good. Let's get to it."

Phug noticed that Gold's statement was not an actual agreement to Phug's terms.

CHAPTER
7

Arrizon walked down the Path of Preferred Payment toward the Central Hall of the *Debenture of Triple-Lined Latinum*, his heart and soul at peace. Trade and commerce went on at stalls and boutiques on either side of the Path. Voices spoke softly, and gentle laughter drifted by him. As he passed by Ferengi, they bowed politely, smiled, and walked on. Words were not needed. They shared the joy that was the Way of Milia.

Turning through the Avenue of Actuaries, he reached the Central Hall, with its Fountains of Ystrad. It was a loving scale re-creation of the Swamp Forest of Arrizon's home district. Gold-rimmed, a disk some fifty meters in diameter, the forest rose up into the atrium of the hall. Benches ringed the public space, with timed credit meters mounted on each. Sweeping around the foliage were the fountains themselves, organic-looking threads, rising to above the canopy of green. The water flowed from the sculpted crystal fountains, falling as fine rain over the trees and fungi. He inhaled deeply of the moist, loamy atmosphere. This was a good day. Arrizon smiled again: they had *all* been good days, since Milia returned.

Near the fountains, he saw and politely acknowledged Nakt and Tyvil, two brothers with whom he had been in a bitter dispute over kevas franchise routes just weeks before. Now, that didn't matter. It was a detail, a curiosity in the greater fabric of the Way of Milia. They nodded back, genuine smiles on their faces.

Soon, he thought, *all Ferengi would know this peace, this contentment.*

As he moved on, seeking a bench to sit on for the allotted period his credits would buy, to fully absorb the ambience of the fountains, he noticed four humans. He approached them. Three of them were, he noted dispassionately, clothed females.

He smiled at them. He was *glad* to see them.

They seemed wary; the tall blond-haired one, carrying a large weapon, spoke quietly to the two dark-haired females and their tall male companion. The male was also armed.

"That will not work here," he informed the male, politely. He turned at this.

"Excuse me?"

"Your weapon. No weapons work here. It is the Way of Milia." He beamed a beatific smile. "We have no need of such things. We are all friends here, all of Milia."

The female with the longer black hair started, "Friend . . . uh . . . ?"

"Arrizon," he prompted helpfully.

"Friend Arrizon," she continued, "we seek the Central Core of your fine ship. Can you help?"

In a grand gesture he indicated the Fountains. "Can there be a greater center than this? It is an expression of all that is glorious on Ferenginar: the rain, the trees, the scent . . . all that binds us, all that makes us Ferengi!" He was lost in the ecstasy of his exhalations.

"I was asking more about a *systems* core. Where the machinery is?"

This brought Arrizon up short. The sheer resonant joy and the beauteous rhythms his heart and soul rang to were interrupted momentarily. A voice in his head said: *She shouldn't be asking about this.* It was, he noted with some confusion, not his own voice.

He shook his head, looked away, raising his arm behind him to wave to them dismissively. "I, ah, can't help you. Sorry, I have to move on now."

He started away, his gait a shuffling uncomfortable one, the Fountains of Ystrad and their attendant joys gone from his mind. He had to find his peace again, commune with Milia.

Gomez watched as the small, nervous Ferengi slunk away. Seconds before he was joy unparalleled; now he was nervous.

"Odd," commented Carol Abramowitz, the ship's cultural specialist. "That's the first negative reaction we've gotten from a Ferengi since we got here."

"I know what you mean," Corsi said. Despite the Ferengi's warning, neither she nor Vance

Hawkins had lowered their phasers. "It's making me nervous."

Gomez sighed. "And Phug's directions are proving less than helpful . . . it's like someone's redesigned elements of this city-ship to deliberately hide the computer core."

"It's like a living representation of the Seventy-Sixth Rule," Corsi said. "'Every once in a while, declare peace. It confuses the hell out of your enemies!'"

Gomez shook her head. "That's the second time you've quoted the Ferengi Rules of Acquisition, Domenica. I'd expect Carol here to know them, but it hardly seems your area of expertise, no offense."

"None taken." Corsi nodded at a passing trader decked in the long coat and gleaming bejeweled headskirt of a Senior Actuary, before continuing. "As far as I'm concerned, there's no difference between the Rules of Acquisition and any other handbook of war—Sun-Tzu's *The Art of War*, Admiral Chekov's *Meditations on a Pre-Surak Vulcan*, the writings of Kahless. That they call their battles 'commerce' is a matter of semantics." She smiled. "Two Hundred Thirty-Ninth Rule: 'Never be afraid to mislabel a product.'"

As they turned into the Row of Restored Antiquities (as Phug's directions indicated) they noticed a short hooded figure, obviously a Ferengi, though he carried himself differently than the others. He held a staff, made of conduit piping, Gomez noted with some curiosity. "Something . . ." she muttered.

"What is it, Commander?" Corsi asked.

"There's something oddly familiar to all this . . . this niceness. Especially that one," she added, pointing to the hooded Ferengi.

The Ferengi then raised his staff, his hood falling back slightly.

Gomez noted with alarm his dead, dark eyes.

CHAPTER
8

David Gold paced the bridge, waiting for word from his away team. There was something that didn't feel right about the whole situation. Something irritatingly familiar, but he couldn't put his finger on it. *Must be getting old,* he thought with a wry smile.

He turned to the aft computer station. "How we doing, Soloman?"

The Bynar's eyes looked up momentarily to acknowledge the captain, then flicked back to the displays. "I have restricted many of the subroutines that the worm has sought to access, though it seems to be learning quickly. I have had to change the encryption sequences every few seconds. It is, oddly, very much like the human game of chess— every move I make is responded to with a counter-move."

"So how are you doing?" Gold asked.

Soloman stared intently at the displays in front of him, allowing himself a small smile. "I have lost perhaps two pawns, but no bishops or knights. My opponent has suffered loss of a rook and four pawns. Metaphorically speaking, of course."

Gold put an encouraging arm on the engineer's shoulder. "My wife always beat me, because I'd go for the queen first. She always got pawns across the board to collapse my second line. Keep up the game, Soloman." He turned to McAllan. "Any word from them yet?"

The tactical officer shook his head. "Not yet, sir. Still five minutes until the designated call-in point. Do you want me to hail them?"

Gold shook his head. "No, no—let's give them the five minutes."

It had taken less than five minutes for the away team to be surrounded.

Several Ferengi in robes had gathered around them. Each of them brandished an apparently hollow length of piping. Gomez recognized them as twenty-millimeter tetracarbide, hi-tensile, low-conductivity thermabore—hardly the most threatening weapon in the galaxy, especially against phasers. Even if that other Ferengi had been right in his statement that the phasers wouldn't work, Gomez had faith in Corsi and Hawkins's ability to take on half a dozen Ferengi with glorified pipes.

There was something about the way they were holding those pipes that was familiar to Gomez as well, but she couldn't put her finger on it.

The blissful traders had looked around to note the scene, but then turned back to their business.

Before Gomez could say anything, a projected

image of a Ferengi appeared before the group. He beamed, and his features were aquiline—*he's almost attractive,* Gomez thought with surprise. She'd never seen a Ferengi with straight teeth. Or such a look of serene contentment.

"Greetings to you, friends. I am the Prophet Milia. Are you of the Way?"

Suddenly, everything clicked in Sonya Gomez's head. The odd sense of familiarity that had been nagging in the back of her head finally came into focus as soon as the serene Ferengi asked about "the Way."

"Yes," she said quickly, "we are."

"My Adjusters were concerned about your inquiries. Such questioning is not of the Way. Being part of the Way of Milia is to be of the whole of Milia." He nodded to them, putting his hand to his chest. *"Joy to you, friends. Peace and contentment will fill you."*

He faded as quickly as he'd appeared, the moment of confrontation having apparently passed. Gomez, however, felt her apprehension growing.

"We," she said, "are in big trouble."

DaiMon Phug paced around the mess hall, occasionally looking up at the quiescent security detail stationed to watch him. He muttered and swore under his breath. Pausing, he turned to the guards. They were both males, thankfully, one a Bajoran male called Loten, the other a human named Foley. Having had his fill of humans, Phug posed his question to the Bajoran.

"When are we getting out of here? Do you know how long I've been cooped up in this room?"

Loten nodded. "About three hours."

"What is taking your people so long?" He shook his head, gesturing wildly with his arms. "Shouldn't have sent females! This stupid human belief in equality is going to be the ruin of your society!"

Suddenly, a connection he'd not previously made linked in his mind.

"Oh, no. They sent *females*." He turned to Loten. "Get me your captain—now!"

"Why?"

"Because your precious away team will be in desperate trouble if I don't."

Loten looked at Foley, who just shrugged. Then the Bajoran tapped his combadge. "Loten to bridge."

"Gold here."

"Sir, the Ferengi says that there's a problem with the away team."

"What kind of problem?"

"He won't say, sir."

"DaiMon, you want to join this conversation?" Gold said tartly.

Phug hesitated. "It's about the nature of what they're going to face over there . . . and about the fact you sent females."

Gold made some kind of noise. *"Why do you Ferengi cling to this barbaric notion of women as second cla—"*

"No!" Phug cut him off. "You don't understand—it's because they are the *only* females on that ship!" Phug ground his teeth, trying to figure out a way to phrase it without revealing any culpability on his own part. "It's to do with the system set up on the city-ship—the, uh, nature of the situation over there—one which," he added quickly, "I will attest before a registered Commerce Authority attorney that I was *wholly* unaware of when I engaged in the transaction!"

"*Spit it out, DaiMon!*" Gold shouted.

"You have to beam them off the *Debenture* right now. It's about to get *very* nasty over there!"

CHAPTER
9

The away team moved on, with several of the cloaked Ferengi following not far behind. Gomez was scanning ahead with her tricorder.

"You said we're in trouble, Commander," Corsi whispered testily, not wanting their pursuers to overhear. "I'd appreciate some details."

"The power source seems to come from this direction," Gomez said. "Of course, we've thought that about six times in the past few hours."

"Commander—"

"Give me a minute, Domenica," Gomez said while still considering the readout on the tricorder. She indicated a narrow corridor to their left. Here, some very young-looking Ferengi had set up stalls. The goods didn't seem to have any theme to them, unlike other similar setups they'd seen on the *Debenture*.

"What is this?" Hawkins asked.

Abramowitz smiled. "What we have here is the Ferengi version of a coming-of-age ritual. When

Ferengi boys first go into business for themselves, they sell off their childhood possessions to give them a starting stake in business."

The ambient noise in this area was even louder than it was in other commerce areas, so it suited Gomez just fine. Even taking into account the fact that Ferengi had superior eavesdropping abilities, she was pretty sure they could have a private conversation here.

"So what's going on, Commander?" Corsi asked irritably.

As if on cue, a blaring alarm sounded out across the halls of the *Debenture*.

"Dammit," Gomez muttered.

The Ferengi started shrieking and screaming, upturning stalls, shattering earthenware, ripping at drapes. Several turned from their wanton destruction and looked in the away team's direction. They were grinning. It was beyond any lascivious leer Gomez had seen on the face of a Ferengi, which was saying a considerable amount.

"Let's move, people," Gomez said. "Corsi, take point."

They moved almost as a single unit, Corsi in the lead as instructed, Gomez and Abramowitz in the middle, Hawkins taking up the rear. They turned the corner into a narrow alley, and watched as the rampaging mob shot past them. Gomez gave out a low gasp of relief, which was suddenly choked off by the figure that stepped from the shadows from among the detritus in the alley. It was one of the hooded Ferengi.

From the diminutive frame came a deep booming voice.

"Why are you not engaged in the Bacchanal? It is the Way of Milia."

"What, you're not calling it the Red Hour anymore?" Gomez asked.

"Huh?" Corsi asked.

Before Gomez could explain, the Ferengi raised the conduit pipe with the open end pointing at the away team.

"You are not of Milia. You must *become*."

Both Corsi and Hawkins raised their weapons to fire—and nothing happened.

The Ferengi's empty pipe welled up with energy that smoked and sparked, firing a charge at Hawkins.

"Agggh!"

As Hawkins slumped to the floor, Corsi leapt over his prone body, swinging her phaser rifle like a baseball bat, knocking down the hooded Ferengi.

Abramowitz crouched by Hawkins. The security guard had been in charge of the portable medikit. She took it from his prone form, opened the tricorder, and ran it over him.

"Okay, a medic I'm not, but his heart rate shouldn't be accelerated, should it?"

"Get away from him, Carol, now!" Gomez called out.

Abramowitz got up just as Hawkins's eyes snapped open, showing an almost glassy blankness. His lips pulled back into a rictus grin.

"Bacchanal!" he shrieked in a voice obviously

not his own measured tones. He grabbed at the cultural specialist.

Before either Corsi or Gomez could react, the expression on Hawkins's face turned to one of surprise and then he slumped to the side, unconscious but with eyes still wide.

They looked into the darkness of the alley behind Hawkins. Another Ferengi stood there, a block of gold-pressed latinum in his hands. He was panting heavily at the effort required to club Hawkins in the head with it.

Corsi was about to return the favor when Gomez stopped her. "No wait, look! He's not like the others."

The Ferengi gave her a withering look. "Oh, you think?"

He slumped against the wall. Gomez noticed his outfit: unlike the other Ferengi they had seen, he was positively scruffy, as though he'd been buried among all this detritus.

"Thank you," she said. "We're indebted to you."

"And I'm already calculating the interest, you can be certain of that. We've got to get you off the streets while this madness goes on. You females are not safe."

Corsi looked suspicious. "What does it profit you to help us?"

He shrugged. "This ship is full of Ferengi all acting . . . polite." He practically sneered the word. "They're completely failing to take advantage of each other. It's a direct violation of the Eighteenth Rule."

Corsi nodded. "'A Ferengi without profit is no Ferengi at all.'"

He looked at Corsi with surprise and respect on his face. "That's right. Anyhow, when I saw you wandering around, I realized that you were an opportunity to resolve this sad, sick situation."

"And looking for a way to gain advantage for yourself?"

He smiled. "Is that so bad?"

Corsi narrowed her gaze. "Ninth Rule: 'Opportunity plus instinct equals profit.' You certainly aren't under this controlling intelligence."

"No, I'm not. C'mon, we need to get out of here." He removed the grille he was leaning against from the wall. "I have a safe area through here."

Corsi looked to Gomez, who nodded. The first officer was grateful that they had found someone not under the influence of this force that hadn't been heard of in almost a century. "Let's go."

"What about Hawkins?" Corsi asked.

Gomez sighed. "If we take him with us, it'll make it all the easier for them to find us. Believe me, as part of the Way of Milia, he'll be okay until we can sort all this out."

They made the security guard as comfortable as possible among the discarded displays and goods in the alleyway, then crawled into the conduit. Corsi sealed the vent behind them as the Ferengi led them through the thin space.

The passageway led into a deep room, where the Ferengi had obviously been hiding for a few days. He gestured for them to sit on cushions he had scattered about the floor.

"Make yourselves as comfortable as you can," the Ferengi said. "My name is Forg."

"Pleasure to meet you, Forg," Gomez said. "So when did DaiMon Phug acquire the Landru computer?"

CHAPTER
10

Gold had Phug brought to his ready room. The DaiMon looked shifty, uncomfortable. He refused to meet Gold's gaze.

"So you're saying that the technology you purchased to administer your systems after you installed the cloak array was from a dubious source?"

Phug looked alarmed. "Dubious? Why, my brother had been married to his aunt's sister—I could trust Caerph as if he were a member of my own family." He paused. "Well, now you mention it . . ."

"My crew is in danger, Phug. I need to know what we're dealing with here!" Gold snapped.

Phug looked concerned. "You mean you didn't beam them back as soon as I told you to? They're still there?"

"Whatever it is that's trying to invade our system has managed to lock out transporters. We can't hail them because they seem to have gone into some kind of shielded environment. So I need to know—exactly what is the situation over there?"

Phug shook his head. "This is bad, this is so bad." He looked up at Gold. "The administration technology was somewhat . . . antiquated. I got it for a good price. Apparently, it had previously been used to operate systems on a small, low-tech world. I figured that for the needs of my ship's cloak array it would be adequate."

"So what went wrong?"

Phug started walking around the room, gesturing wildly. "Well, at first, nothing. Then, my engineers started noticing that it began to interface with the other systems, in ways that just didn't make any sense. Before long, it had taken total control of the whole ship.

"Initially, that wasn't too bad. It meant I could lay off about a dozen maintenance staff. And let me tell you, on a ship that size, the opportunities to maximize the margins are difficult to find. Then, I started getting reports of all these—incidents."

"Violent incidents?" asked Gold.

"No, just the opposite. Everyone was being . . . pleasant to each other." He shuddered at the word *pleasant* as though it were something base and deviant. "Before long, everyone on the station was acting in an orderly, caring way." A further shudder, then he raised his hand, as though trying to push the very thoughts away. "And then, *he* came. *Milia.*"

"I'm afraid the significance of that name escapes me, DaiMon," Gold said dryly.

"He is our darkest legend, Captain. A Ferengi unlike any other. He preached such values as peace, love, and understanding. This—this *freak* spoke of sharing, of being of a benevolent society. Naturally he suffered a legendarily brutal execution, as did his heretic followers." Phug sighed.

"When was this?" Gold asked.

"Several thousand years ago. Why?"

Gold was confused. "So how can he be 'back' now?"

The edge of fear was back in Phug's voice. "I don't know, Captain, but I just wish he'd return to wherever it was he came from. He has changed some of our finest merchants into his 'keepers of order.' Any who speak out against Milia are absorbed into the whole. It started so gradually— then the whole ship was taken over, almost before I'd registered what was happening. I barely escaped with my sanity."

"So why are you so worried about my crew?"

"Because, for some reason, this 'peace and love' cult sporadically erupts into violence and lust. They call it the Bacchanal. And your crewmembers are the only women on the station!"

"Bacchanal?" Gold repeated, wondering why a Ferengi would spontaneously erupt into behavior named for the Greek god of wine and celebration, Bacchus.

Then he remembered something from old Starfleet records—specifically the early days of the S.C.E. "Phug—this computer of yours. Does it have a name?"

*   *   *

In Forg's hideaway, the away team were being told the same story—Gomez nodding as the details emerged, fitting the pattern she knew from the historical record.

"On Beta III about a hundred years ago, the crew of the *Enterprise* encountered a planet that had become stultified as a low-level agrarian society. The world computer, Landru, maintained this static model for several thousand years. Everyone happy, everything calm and settled."

"Then what happened out there with 'Bacchanal'? That hardly seems to fit," asked Corsi, constantly checking all the exits to the room as she spoke. She was sure they'd be invaded by a horde of smiling Ferengi any minute. . . .

Gomez shrugged. "There had to be a release of negative emotions, baser desires. For a period, these model citizens indulged in all kinds of lasciviousness, wanton destruction, random insanity. They called it 'Red Hour.' This happened every few months."

Forg looked surprised. "This is the third Bacchanal in the past four weeks!"

Corsi gave him a withering glance. "Obviously, Ferengi have far more negative emotions than mere 'hew-mons.'"

Abramowitz looked at Forg. "How come you escaped all this?"

Forg shrugged. "I was attacked by one of the Adjusters—a spice-master called Zin, who I'd had dealings with. I was trying to escape the ship when he cornered me. I thought that was it . . . but it seems the attack didn't affect me as it did your dark-skinned friend. I was linked into the whole 'Milia' harmony briefly, then shook free. I took to hiding—"

There was a sound by one of the other access points in the room. Everyone looked around; Corsi raised her useless phaser rifle at the approaching figures. *Damn,* she thought, *we're completely cornered and my only backup is either unconscious or has woken up and is living out a Ferengi spree of wanton indulgence in an alleyway. . . .*

Forg then walked past her, waving for her to stand down. "Don't worry—I know those footfalls." He shouted ahead. "Hey! It's okay, they're here to help us!"

Two Ferengi cautiously walked into the storeroom, warily checking out the Starfleet people.

Forg introduced them. "These Ferengi are brothers, Ainoc and Aylai. Like me they seem to be immune to the Adjusters' beams. We have to hide out here, while the madness of Bacchanal passes."

Ainoc looked sheepish.

Forg stared at him. "What did you do?"

Ainoc grinned. "Well, as they were all wrecking their stalls and generally treating property in a vile and disrespectful manner, we carefully reallocated resources within our portfolio."

"Much as I hate to interrupt the financial report," Gomez said tightly, "we have a situation here, and you're the only people who can help us. We have to find the computer core of this ship, and disable it."

Aylai nodded emphatically. "That's fine with

us. If I never see Milia's smiling face again. . . ."

"This Milia," Abramowitz said—and the three Ferengi shuddered at the name—"is some kind of, what—prophet in Ferengi history? I've never heard of him."

"No reason you should, human," Aylai said. "He was a deviant who proposed cooperation—exactly the type of society that is breaking out here like some kind of disease."

Gomez nodded. "So when the system went online, it did as Landru had before: it looked for an ideal situation in your databanks and created a symbol of that 'best' time, taking on the personality and appearance of Milia himself."

"It's doing more than that," Ainoc said. "Apparently we won't be alone in this 'joy.' The Adjusters are taking the ship to Ferenginar—and they plan to 'convert' all the ships they meet along the way."

Corsi cocked the useless rifle—an instinctive gesture, but one that made her feel better nonetheless. "So this is the situation in a nutshell: your DaiMon purchases a hundred-year-old computer to run his ship. Said computer proceeds to take over the ship, in the process re-creating a Ferengi heretic who preaches a commune mentality subservient to his computer-driven idea of 'the Whole.' Said prophet is now determined to convert the whole galaxy to this system of belief—probably starting with the *da Vinci*, if you're right about them converting any ship they meet along the way. And he has a cloaked vessel that can strike anywhere in the Alpha Quadrant to do this."

"I'd say that sums it up," Gomez said grimly.

"And we're here to seek an engineering solution to all this?"

There was a pause, then Gomez smiled. "Actually, I believe Captain Kirk's solution on Beta III a hundred years ago was a classic engineering solution."

"Which was?" asked Forg.

"Pull the plug."

CHAPTER
11

The face of Captain Montgomery Scott came into focus as the Starfleet logo faded on Captain Gold's personal screen.

"You have a wee problem, David?"

"Afraid so, Scotty. Looks like we dug up another one of your old adventures. Remember Landru?"

Scott sighed. *"Aye, I remember bein' stuck on the* Enterprise, *while the bloody computer shot heat beams at us. If Captain Kirk hadna defeated Landru, our ship would have been sliced into charred strips."*

"Well, Landru just resurfaced—on a Ferengi ship." Quickly, Gold filled Scotty in.

Shaking his head, Scott said, *"Unbelievable, those Ferengi. Although I will admit that it's odd that you of all people came across it, considerin' that the S.C.E. as we know it today came about in the aftermath of that old mission to Beta III."*

"I remember," Gold said. The team that had gone in to put Beta III back together after

Landru's deactivation was a prototype of the current model for the Starfleet Corps of Engineers.

Gold continued. "Unfortunately, I can't get at our computer logs right now. It's all Soloman can do to keep us from being taken over. So I need to know how Captain Kirk dealt with the computer back then."

Scott smiled. *"He reasoned with it. He an' Mr. Spock convinced it that its very existence was contrary to its programming. The bampot machine then upped and destroyed itself."*

Gold raised an eyebrow at this. "They talked it to death?"

"Somethin' like that, aye. It believed itself to be the embodiment of its creator, the original Landru. When it realized it had so violated his intentions in creating a peaceful society, almost out of shame it shut itself down. I don't know if that'll work here, though."

The Bacchanal had passed; the streets and avenues of the *Debenture* were littered with wreckage and detritus. Walking through the Boulevard of Nectar and Sustenance (a varied collection of restaurants and bars, the wares of which were spilled and spoiled across the broad avenues of the ship), the away team and their Ferengi companions nodded and acknowledged the now-calm followers of Milia.

Speaking as softly as he could, Forg said, "It won't be long before Milia realizes what we're doing. There are about two thousand Ferengi on this vessel. What do you think about those odds?"

"I think that we'll deal with that if and when we have to." Gomez tapped her combadge. "Gomez to *da Vinci*."

The captain's voice sounded full of relief. *"Good to hear from you, finally, Gomez."*

"Good to be heard, Captain. We've been stuck in a shielded area. I think you should know what's been happening here—"

"Phug was finally forthcoming about that. He told me all about Landru."

"Tell Phug he has the lobes of a female!" commented Forg.

"Who's with you?" asked Gold as Corsi shot Forg a look.

"We've found a few who aren't followers of Milia, sir," Gomez said. "They kept us safe when the Ferengi version of the Red Hour hit."

"Good. Status?"

"We lost Hawkins to the Milians. One of the Ferengi knocked him unconscious. If we're lucky he'll stay out of it until we can resolve the situation. They also don't intend to limit the return of Milia to just this ship."

Gold replied, *"I know. As it happens, we just heard from Ferenginar. Apparently this 'Milia' has told them he's on the way—they're none too happy about the prospect. We need to resolve this situation swiftly."*

"We're on it, sir."

In the Halls of Commerce on Ferenginar, on the Atrium of Announcements, the babble of voices had hit a higher pitch than had been heard since the legendary dark days of the Great Monetary Collapse.

"Silence!" shouted Senior Adjuster Brumm, a middle-aged Ferengi with fine, wrinkled lobes.

He had been dragged from having these fine lobes massaged by a group of diplomatic hand-maidens from Wrigley's Pleasure Planet. They were currently visiting to negotiate trading and vacation rates with the Ferenginar Alliance. This was his own personal economic project to promote Ferengi interests on worlds of particular sybaritic interest. Pleasure and commerce were forever linked in Ferengi culture.

Forever, he thought mournfully. *Won't be much longer when Milia comes here. . . .*

Finally the hubbub quieted down. They looked up at the disheveled Adjuster. "Thank you."

"Tell us it's not true!" yelled Bromidge, an elderly Ferengi. Brumm knew that Bromidge's interests included hard-fought spice and herbs routes into the Gamma Quadrant. Those deals had drained three of his sons' fortunes—a detail that Bromidge had kept from his offspring, and of which they would remain unaware until the Great Audit took their father away—until this horrific turn of events had occurred and threatened the death knell of Ferengi culture.

Unfortunately, the Senior Adjuster was not in a position to give succor to the massed hordes of Ferengi businessmen gathered before him.

"It is as we have all seen on our screens. The great heretic Milia is returning. These are not some aberrant broadcasts of a cunning plan to undermine Ferengi stocks and create a rash of panic selling . . . ." He paused, wondering why he hadn't considered this idea himself, as did most in the hall (apart from Bromidge, who was no doubt calculating how thinly he'd have to be sliced to pay off his sons). Brumm continued, ". . . deplorable as that would be. No, it really is a re-creation of Milia. And he's coming here."

The gasp rang through the hall. The chattering and swearing came louder than before, then the accusations started flying.

"It's a judgment! If we hadn't gone down the path dictated by Grand Nagus Zek, this would never be happening!"

"Women in clothes! It was a sign of the Great Liquidation!"

"Our latinum is water, our gold is mud! We've strayed!"

"Ahem."

They all turned to see the two figures that now stood next to Brumm. One was Rom—a quite ordinary-looking Ferengi wrapped in the robes of the Grand Nagus, and still not looking comfortable in them even after several months in the role. Next to him stood a statuesque Bajoran female: his wife Leeta, no less stunning for being completely clothed. Brumm, still with the memories of the ambassadors of Wrigley lingering in his mind, had to admit they'd have a ways to go to match her presence.

"Pray silence for your Grand Nagus, Rom!" he cried.

Rom stepped forward. "Uh, hi, everyone. I just

thought you all should know that I've spoken to my friends in the Federation and they've sent out a starship to deal with this situation."

There was a mixture of cheers and mumbling. The Federation and Ferenginar had always had a strained relationship, with confusion, duplicity, and outright double-dealing making up so much of the history between them. One voice cried out, attempting to rally them.

"I bet they've sent the *Enterprise!* The human Picard has proved a worthy adversary to Ferengi in the past! He's the one to stop this heretic!"

There were more cheers, the Ferengi warming to the theme.

"Uh, no, actually," admitted Rom.

The same one—Brumm finally recognized him as Quinton, a young idealistic Ferengi who'd idolized Zek, and saw links with the Federation as the way ahead—thought for a second, as the worried mumbling returned, then brightly exclaimed: "Captain Sisko and the *Defiant!* He is our champion!"

More cheers responded to this, though Brumm knew that Sisko had, in fact, disappeared after the Dominion War ended and his space station was now run by a Bajoran female who was not (in Brumm's opinion) nearly as stunning as the Nagus's wife.

Rom replied, "Uh, no—Captain Sisko is, uh, unavailable now. But it is a great leader and a fantastic ship! Captain Gold of the *da Vinci!*"

Quinton looked baffled by the name, then thought better of his confusion and so cried out,

"Hooray for Captain Gold!" Other Ferengi joined in. The cheering rallied them.

Brumm turned to Rom, and in a soft voice asked, "Who?"

Rom smiled, a warm generous grin. "My son liked him. He said he seemed like a very nice man."

Brumm blinked. "Oh. Well, there we go."

Rom raised the Cane of the Grand Nagus. "Carry on trading! Everything will be all right!"

Rom and Leeta left, waving to the amassed businessmen. Brumm gave a polite nod, and headed back to his chambers. *We're entrusting the whole future of our civilization to a human the Grand Nagus's son thinks is "nice." We're doomed. . . .*

CHAPTER
12

The away team and their Ferengi hosts found themselves up against stacked boarding and detritus, completely out of keeping with the layout of the surrounding boutiques and clothing stores on the Level of the Golden Measure.

"Now *that* looks promising," Corsi muttered.

Gomez scanned with her tricorder. The Ferengi who had fallen into the Way of Milia paid her no mind now that the Bacchanal had ended.

"There's something beyond all this debris," she said. "A very powerful energy signal."

Corsi started pulling off boards and other objects, which Gomez recognized as various pieces of shop displays—garment racks, book display stands, tables.

As she dismantled, a familiar voice said, "Health to us all, fellow of the Way of Milia. What are you doing, citizen?"

The *da Vinci* security chief turned to see Vance Hawkins, still with the remains of the trash he'd fallen into hanging from his uniform. On his face was the biggest grin Gomez had ever seen, and, given how much time she'd spent in Kieran Duffy's company, this was going some. Vance was usually a quiet, reserved sort; when he did smile, it was a small, pleasant one, and his eyes generally betrayed a certain intelligence. This grin, however, was eerie, the eyes above it dead.

"Knitting fish," Corsi replied, and Gomez nodded with approval. Kirk and his crew had confused Landru's minions by giving inappropriate responses to requests, and Gomez had ordered them all to try this when challenged.

It seemed to have the desired effect—Hawkins blinked twice at the nonsequitur, and looked into the air as though responding to some unheard voice. He turned back to Corsi. The grin was still there, but it now looked forced and uncertain.

"Is this the Will of Milia? I do not think you are acting in the best interests of the whole."

"Cheese gets soft in Norway," Gomez said. She turned to Abramowitz, hoping she'd get the idea.

She did; unfortunately that wasn't the problem. Carol Abramowitz, an academic without equal, froze at the thought of speaking in nonsense.

"I—I—I—dictate in Spanish wh-when underwater." She shot Gomez a panicked look. *Is that okay?* she mouthed.

Gomez nodded encouragingly. *Confused the heck out of me,* she thought.

Hawkins looked among the three women. Whatever voices were talking to him were obviously debating hard. Abramowitz took the moment's delay to reach into the emergency medikit to ready a hypospray. She slowly walked behind the guard, ready to send him back to sleep.

Before she could react, his arm struck out behind him, sending her sprawling.

"Carol!" cried out Gomez, running to her side. Hawkins turned to follow her, obviously intent on carrying on the Will of Milia with extreme prejudice.

Corsi stood poised with a heavy metal stand obviously designed to show off Ferengi headskirts to best effect. Balanced on her left foot, she swung the display, smashing her subordinate clean across the face. He fell solidly like an oak.

"Nice to see the subtle approach still works," she muttered under her breath. She went over to help Gomez assist Abramowitz to her feet. "If you want to try that hypospray again, I think you'll find your patient's a little more sedate."

Ainoc started spluttering, "Starfleet! Starfleet! We've got a problem!"

The three turned to see that the shopkeepers and customers had started to take notice of them. The placid Ferengi began picking up the bits of rubble discarded by Corsi. There were dozens of Ferengi, and they weren't going to stop. The remaining rubble and shop display detritus blocked the only route out.

In the air in front of them, the figure of Milia appeared again, a pained expression of reproof on his face.

"You seek to harm Milia. To harm the whole, the way of Milia. This cannot be allowed."

Gomez steeled herself. *There has to be a way out of this*, she thought. Her engineer's mind refused to accept that they couldn't think their way to a solution.

Then Corsi tapped her on the shoulder. To Gomez's abject shock, the no-nonsense, by-the-book security chief had a smile on her face.

"I have an idea, Commander. Trust me?"

Gomez mulled for half a second. She'd served with Corsi for many months now, and had indeed learned to trust her instincts. Bereft of any ideas of her own, she nodded, wondering what Corsi had in mind.

Corsi walked up to the holo-image, and did the last thing Gomez expected to see.

She bowed deferentially and said, "Great Milia, we surrender."

Gomez shot Corsi a look of surprise—the Ferengi and Abramowitz did likewise, but they were in complete shock.

"We are part of a mighty vessel," Corsi said. "It has many who would benefit from the joining with your Way. Take us into your presence, that we may bring forth our crewmates!"

Gomez smiled, finally getting it. *Let's hope we live to see this through*, she thought. She gave Abramowitz and the Ferengi a reassuring nod. Carol looked placated, the Ferengi somewhat less so, but they made no move against them, either.

Milia beamed beatifically. *"Then let it be so."* He gestured for the Ferengi to dismantle the rubble wall. They made short work of it.

Total hive mind, thought Gomez. *Their individ-*

ual identity subsumed to the whole. Almost Borg-like.

Ferengi Borg. There's an image I didn't need. . . .

Within minutes, the wreckage was removed, the path to the core cleared. Gomez didn't know the Rules of Acquisition, but she did know one of Corsi's other handbooks: *The Art of War* by Sun-Tzu. Right now they were on what Sun-Tzu would call "entangling ground." If the enemy was not prepared for you, you would win; if the enemy *was* prepared, though, and you failed to defeat him, disaster would ensue.

The path opened out into a vast computer hub. The systems that had once been independent of the Landru mechanism were all linked now through conduits and systems carriers. Some Gomez recognized; some she was at a loss to explain how they could still operate. The actual computer unit was an unprepossessing gray block, adorned with chip blocks of reds, whites, and yellows. The technology was so outdated, she half-expected there to actually be a cable running into a wall socket—or maybe a hamster on a wheel powering the whole thing.

The holo-image of Milia that had led them and their entourage of at least fifty Ferengi into this hall turned to the away team. On either side of the team stood diminutive Adjusters, their cloaks darkening their faces.

"Here you stand within the proud beating heart of the Way of Milia. This vessel will reach Ferenginar and all races throughout the galaxy, bringing them to the family, to the Way itself." He gestured toward

Corsi. *"It is your honor to be the first ship to go with joy."*

Corsi nodded respectfully, stepping forward, her hand reaching out to the ancient computer core. She tapped it gently. "Milia is good," she said.

"Step away from the holy sepulcher, citizen," intoned the deep voice from the nearest Adjuster.

She bowed deferentially. "I meant no disrespect."

Never thought I'd live to see this, Gomez thought with an internal smile. *I just hope I've read her intentions right. . . .*

"Gomez to da Vinci."

Kieran Duffy had never in his life been so relieved to hear Sonnie's voice. *Well, okay, there was when I found her on Sarindar, but this is a very, very close second.*

There was, however, something odd about her voice. . . .

"Da Vinci here," Gold said. "Report."

"We have decided to follow the Way of Milia, Captain, and invite you to join us in this holy, joyous path."

Duffy felt his world spin away from him. Sonnie had somehow fallen under the power of this millennia-old device. He felt a sickening feeling that they'd just lost.

At the back of the bridge, Phug started cursing and spluttering. "Stupid humans! Pwagh! You have failed! You have doomed us all! I told you! I told you!"

"We want you, your wife Rachel, and everyone else on the ship to join us in the Way, Captain."

Duffy's world spun right back into place. Sonnie knew quite well that Gold's wife was back home on Earth. Someone under the influence, so to speak, wouldn't have been able to lie. He grinned at Gold, who grinned right back.

"I shall take your generous offer under advisement, Commander," Gold said. "Tell me where might we find you currently. Your signal's coming from an area we're having problems getting a fix on."

"We are here in the very heart of the Way, sir. Standing side by side with Milia himself."

"Aha. I see. How do you suggest we proceed?"

Gomez looked around the room, all eyes expectantly on her. *We're going to have to time this just right,* she thought, *or we'll all become Milians for real.*

"Captain, can you operate transporters yet?" she said in the languid voice she'd adopted for the purpose.

"No—the computer worm is still blocking that and all defense systems."

"Then, tell Soloman to stop fighting it, sir. Allow the *da Vinci* to become one with the mighty Milia."

There was a second's pause.

"Are you sure about this, Gomez?"

"Yes, sir!" She grinned wildly, looking at the approving grins on all the Ferengi around her. "Think of it as . . . Masada. You know, that great tale you told me, of personal sacrifice?"

"Masada? But—one second, Commander."

Another pause. The Ferengi continued to grin beatifically. Milia turned to Gomez. *"Why does your captain delay?"*

"I think you'll find he needs you to show your openness and all-embracing love. Let his ship sense where we are. Diminish your shields slightly. It would be a noble gesture."

"It shall be so."

Ina's displays lit up, identifying the position of the away team. "We've got a fix on them, sir," Duffy said, standing over the Bajoran ops officer. "Now what?"

"Open hailing frequencies again. I think I know what they're planning, but I need to be sure."

"Dead dead dead," muttered Phug.

"Gold here, Commander. We've considered your invitation. I need more clarification on the 'Masada' analogy . . . who among you is to carry out this great deed?"

Gomez hoped the relief she felt didn't show on her face. *He got it.* They still needed to play this carefully, though.

"Lt. Commander Corsi, sir. When you're ready."

Gold gave a throat-cutting gesture to McAllan to end the transmission, then tapped the intercom on his chair. "Transporter room, lock onto Corsi and energize on my mark."

From the transporter room, Chief Feliciano said, *"Aye, sir."*

Gold then got up and walked to Soloman's station.

"What are they planning, sir?" the Bynar asked.

Phug responded before Gold could. "That we're all going to be sold into slavery, to the brainless ways of the joy brigade down there!"

Gold smiled calmly at the Ferengi. "Watch and learn, DaiMon Phug." Turning back to the Bynar, he said, "Soloman, prepare to put your king into checkmate."

"Sir?"

"We'll have a split second when the system becomes completely invaded, but before we lose control, when we can carry out Gomez's 'Masada' play."

The look on Milia's face took on an even more beatific aura. *"They are stopping the fight! They are allowing the love and joy of Milia to—"*

He never got to finish. Behind the crowd, the familiar whine of a transporter beam could be heard. On the *da Vinci*, they had locked onto Corsi—or, more precisely, Corsi's combadge—and energized. Except, of course, Corsi's combadge wasn't attached to her uniform, as she had placed it on the computer that thought of itself as Milia moments earlier.

The holo-image vanished as the physical machine disappeared. The massed Ferengi initially stood stunned, then started looking warily around at each other, backing away from the group.

Forg ran up to Gomez and Corsi. "What did you do?"

"Well, I didn't think we could beat Milia with weapons," Corsi said, "so we had to come up with a different approach."

"And one *worthy* of a Ferengi!" gushed Ainoc. He and his brother had come to join the group. "So devious, so sneaky! To convince the customer you're buying his goods, when in fact you plan to steal his whole warehouse!"

Aylai strummed his fingers against his uneven, green teeth. "Now, which Rule is that?"

Gomez raised a hand. "Please. No more Rules." She tapped her combadge. "Status, Captain?"

"Feliciano beamed the computer core into deep space. As soon as we did, the worm ceased trying to take over the ship. Good plan, Commander."

"It was Corsi, sir. I just followed her lead."

"And it's good to know you actually listen to the ramblings of a doting grandfather . . . that whole 'Masada' conversation we had this morning."

"Yes, sir, I thought you'd appreciate the 'sacrifice rather than fall to slavery' idea."

"Only here, you 'sacrificed' the enslaver."

She nodded happily, as the first fights broke out among the Ferengi behind her.

Five long days passed. The now core-less *Debenture* had been dragged by tractor beam to Starbase 96. The powerless computer core was held in stasis, under guard in the *da Vinci*'s cargo hold.

The vast cleanup operation had begun—there were many shopowners who found they'd carried out transactions for weeks in a fair and equitable way, and consequently were low on resources. DaiMon Phug had sold his controlling share in the vessel to Forg. Under Ferengi law, leaving the vessel as he had was tantamount to abandoning control, and therefore making it open to salvage rights. In a lingering nod to the spirit of Milia, he had allowed Phug to keep his wardrobe of fine silks (none of which fit the taller, less rotund Forg).

The crew of the *da Vinci* had been over to assist in maintaining life-support systems. Fabian Stevens had noted that the systems were of a type that wasn't supposed to be on the market—indeed, that both the Romulans and the Klingons considered possession of those systems to be tantamount to a declaration of war. Consequently, they were impounded and stored in the cargo hold along with the Landru/Milia computer, pending an investigation—one that Phug was not looking forward to. Already, he was trying to figure out ways to make Forg responsible for it.

Hawkins was taken off duty for a few days, recovering from a severe concussion. He announced to Emmett, who treated him, and to anyone else who came into sickbay that in the past few months he'd been shot twice, and now clubbed on the head twice while acting like a lustfilled savage, and he was, dammit, taking some shore leave. Corsi—who did not apologize for being responsible for half of the concussion, having viewed it as simply doing her duty—granted the leave.

* * *

Gold sat in his ready room, the diminutive Klingon language teacher pacing back and forth on the desk.

"Again!"

Gold looked down. "Hmm?" He realized he hadn't been listening. He'd been too busy mulling over the events of the past few days. How the saga of his people from ancient history still had lessons in life today. Of how it was all too easy to listen to a machine, and follow the path of least resistance.

"Well?" The Klingon had his hands on his hips, glaring up at Gold.

"If I want to talk Klingon, I'll do it with a real one," he announced, canceling the program.

As the Klingon disappeared in a puff of photons, he called the bridge and had McAllan put a communication through to Esther on Qo'noS. He would tell her how she'd indirectly inspired his crew, and ask her how it was going with Khor. . . .

PAST LIFE

Robert Greenberger

CHAPTER
1

David Gold, captain of the *U.S.S. da Vinci*, liked his morning routines. He'd pamper himself a little as he got out of his bed and prepared for the new day. He would always make sure to check his computer for official communiqués, then personal notes, as he sipped a hot cup of coffee, usually humming a little something. Most mornings that meant there was something from home. After all, with a wife, children, grandchildren, and great-grandchildren, some-one was usually sending him a note to stay in touch. Everyone seemed to be leading such busy lives; he longed to be beside them all, especially his wife, Rachel.

There was also the thrill of command and pro-found responsibility that came with it. It gave him a thrill and fulfillment like nothing else. When people questioned the long-distance marriage between him and the Earth-based rabbi, he explained that it was both his family and his command together that made his life worth living. He couldn't imagine life without both.

The last part of the routine, and in some ways the best, was the short walk from his cabin to the bridge, accompanied by his first officer, Sonya Gomez. He was not sure how this developed but it pleased him that it had continued mission after mission. She was shorter than the captain and her smile seemed to make the corridors a little brighter.

As usual, she was promptly by his door and greeted him with that electric smile. He always returned it, good night's sleep or not. He gestured for her to enter his small cabin as he shut down his desktop screen.

"Chatter from the fleet looked light today," he commented.

"Calm before the storm," Gomez said with a shrug.

"*Oy*, I hope not," he continued. "We've got an overdue shore leave coming up in two weeks."

"And you're having that big family gathering, right?"

"You bet," the captain said, warming to the notion of going home. "But first, we have quarterly roster review coming up and I was hoping to use the lull to spend a little more time with the crew. For example, I've barely talked to Hawkins since he returned from shore leave."

"Sir, that was just two days ago," Gomez said. She stood expectantly, and Gold was obvious in his hesitation.

Gold considered that Vance Hawkins, of all his

personnel, had been the most banged-up, complete with various wounds and concussions, the last on the Ferengi vessel *Debenture*, which earned him the much-needed shore leave. But he was merely stalling and finally turned to his first officer.

"Which reminds me," the captain said, trying to sound casual. "I've been meaning to ask you . . . has Dr. Lense seemed all right to you?"

She knitted her brows together in thought. It lasted only a moment and then she shook her head. "Elizabeth seems fine to me. Why?"

Now it took Gold a moment before commenting. Such talk always made him uncomfortable, especially without hard facts. "I'm not sure. But she seems awfully reliant on Emmett these days."

"Sometimes we do get busy and isn't that what the EMH was for?"

"Perhaps," he replied, clearly unhappy with the notion. Emergency Medical Hologram or not, the captain was certain Lense had a problem.

Then he shook his head. "Never mind, Commander, let's get under way." He gestured toward the door and she went through first. Together, in companionable silence, they wandered toward the turbolift.

"You should know that we did receive one note that Starbase 92 intercepted a squad of Nausicaan raiders trying to stop a Cardassian relief convoy."

Gold slowed and looked in surprise at Gomez.

"That wasn't in the official report this morning. How did . . . wait, Starbase 92?"

They stepped into the turbolift and Gomez nodded in confirmation. "The one where Anthony is stationed."

"So we know this from Lieutenant Commander Mark, not official channels?"

"Right. Anthony was heavily involved in the mission and sent off a note to Bart last night."

"Nice to have boyfriends in all the right places," Gold said with a smile. "Is he all right?"

"A little shaken to see such heavy action after a long lull," she replied. "But Bart says he's fine."

The doors snapped open and Gold hurried to his chair, eager to see what the day held. As always, and despite Gold's best efforts to get him to stop, his by-the-book tactical officer David McAllan said, "Captain on the bridge."

"Good morning, all," he said as he settled into the command seat. Alpha shift was in place and all seemed serene on the *Saber*-class starship's bridge. A flurry of replies came his way and then mostly silence.

Minutes later, a beep behind him indicated an incoming transmission. *Be careful what you wish for,* he reminded himself before swiveling about to face McAllan. He cocked an eyebrow and looked expectantly at the lieutenant. McAllan looked directly at him, his brown eyes intense. "It's Admiral Ross, sir."

Most of their communications came directly from Montgomery Scott, the Starfleet Corps of Engineers' liaison to the admiralty, so having an admiral call was unusual. Gold straightened himself in the chair and signaled for the main screen to be activated. In seconds, the hangdog face of

Admiral William Ross faced him. Ross was an excellent commanding officer, with one of the best reputations at command. In the wake of the Dominion War and the Iconian gateways incident, Gold had hoped Ross would get a break, but apparently not. Although the captain was older, Ross seemed the more worn down, but the admiralty could do that to anyone, Gold thought.

"Good morning, Admiral," Gold said with a smile.

"Captain, it's nice to see you again," Ross replied. *"I need to divert you to Evora, which is approximately half a day from your position."*

"I can't place the world," Gold admitted.

"It's a protectorate, brought in toward the end of the Dominion War. They've had warp capabilities only a few years and are still getting to know their galactic neighbors."

"How can we help?"

"Their society has been through a lot in a short time, Captain. First, they discover they are not alone in space. Then, they come to us for protection during a rather bleak time. Now, their faith has been shaken."

Gold's eyes narrowed. "How so?" he asked.

"A few days back, one of their archaeological digs came across something high-tech but dating back over one hundred thousand years. It's clearly not from their civilization, and probably not from their world. It's got some of them scared, and the regent, a woman named Cuzar, has asked for our expertise in finding out the truth. You're the closest in the sector, so you're up. Tread gently here, David. Depending

upon what you find there, it could rewrite their history."

"Of course, Admiral, we'll be careful. We'll study up on them en route to be prepared."

"*There's not a lot documented,*" Ross admitted. "*Once the war ended, they kept to themselves and we've been stretched so thin that we haven't had time to send another envoy ship. That is, until now.*"

"We won't disappoint you," Gold said by way of closing. Ross nodded and cut the transmission from his end. The main viewer reverted to an image of the streaking stars as seen in warp space. The captain looked around the bridge to see that Carol Abramowitz, the ship's cultural specialist, had joined the normal bridge complement. He presumed Gomez had summoned her the moment the mission became clear. The trim, dark-haired woman turned her attention from the viewscreen to the captain.

"He's right, sir," she began. "The computer has little more than technical specs. The only Federation personnel to actually meet with them were Captain Picard and the *Enterprise* crew, right after their induction a year and a half ago. Even so, it was a very brief meeting—the *Enterprise* had to cut the ceremony short for another mission. Everything prior to that was handled via subspace."

"Okay, one thing at a time," Gold said. "Wong, set course for Evora, warp six."

"Aye, sir," said the conn officer.

"Gomez, put your team together."

"Sir," Abramowitz said before Gomez could

speak, "I recommend you be on the initial team. The Evorans are big on protocol, and I think the captain should be present for the first meeting."

Gold looked at Gomez and smiled. "Think Duffy's ready for the big chair again?"

"I'm sure he'll be fine," Gomez said, returning the smile. Kieran Duffy, the *da Vinci*'s second officer, had been left in charge of the ship during what should have been a routine salvage mission that almost turned into a war with the Tholian Assembly.

"Good. Have Corsi send someone from security—but not her. With you and I both off-ship, I'd rather she stay on board with Duffy."

CHAPTER
2

In a matter of hours, his crew had prepped themselves as best they could on the race. Gold asked Abramowitz back to the bridge for a briefing. She reported quickly, padd in hand.

"World population is only three hundred million, sir," she began. "They are not a long-lived race; lifespans seem to reach only into the fifties or sixties. From what we can tell, they have been unified under one planetary government for at least three generations. Oh, and they're vegetarian by nature. They have ritualized greetings, but beyond that seem fairly casual."

"Interesting," Gold said, watching a small orb grow in size as the starship hurtled toward its next stop. "Level of technology?"

"Not terribly advanced, maybe the equivalent of twenty-second-century Earth."

"Without the recovery from global war?"

Carol shook her head, her hair never moving so much as a strand. "We don't know much about their history, sir. From all indications, they were rushed into the fold to keep them from the Dominion. I gather we were looking to protect as many races as possible while building our strength along the edges of Federation space."

"Too true." Gold thought back to those dark days. He was busy during the war, concerned on more than one occasion that the Federation might not be recognizable when the conflict finally ended. In some ways, those were heady times. In other ways, he was amazed that he'd escaped intact at all. *And of course, some of us didn't,* he thought, remembering good people like Chan Okha and Commander Salek, who were killed in action.

"Evora coming on screen," Ina Mar, the Bajoran operations officer, reported. Gold, Abramowitz, and the others immediately looked up. Evora was a small brown-green world, denser than Earth with a slightly heavier gravity. Interestingly, the *da Vinci* was the first starship to orbit the world—the ceremony on the *Enterprise* was held in interstellar space—so Gold assigned Ina and Duffy the task of making a thorough survey of the planet for Starfleet.

As they began their work, Gold headed off for the transporter room. On the way, he encountered Bart Faulwell. The captain slowed his gait and greeted the linguist. "Is Anthony all right?"

Bart blinked at the question but smiled and nodded. "Yes, he is, sir, thank you for asking."

"Nausicaans are a pretty brutal bunch, so if he got away without physical injury, he can consider himself lucky."

"He sounded that way in the message," Bart said, sounding happy, albeit a little distracted.

"Give him my best the next time you write," the captain said. Bart smiled and resumed his path while the captain turned back toward the transporter room.

Present in the small room were Gomez, Abramowitz, and Hawkins, as well as Transporter Chief Feliciano and Corsi, who was there to see them off. She seemed to be fretting over being left behind.

However, Gold was not surprised that she had tapped Hawkins. After all, he was just back from leave, so that would put his name at the top of the duty roster. To the broad-shouldered guard, the captain said, "Had a nice trip?"

Hawkins blinked in surprise at the question, then nodded. "Very good, yes, sir."

"Good."

Abramowitz walked up to him. "The Evoran greeting is *yew-cheen chef-faw.*"

Gold practiced it twice and nodded. Carol made a face at him and Gold cocked an eyebrow in her direction.

"The emphasis should be on the *faw,*" she told him.

The captain made a face of annoyance but practiced it twice more, each time looking at his cultural specialist for approval. She smiled, indicating he got it right.

"All right, then. I expect this first meeting to take no longer than an hour," Gold said to his security chief. She nodded, a look of intensity remaining in her eyes. Although Duffy was left in command, Corsi would no doubt be ready to fire phasers at the first sign of trouble. "We'll see if we can bring you back a souvenir," Gold added as he, Gomez, Abramowitz, and Hawkins took their positions. With a nod to Feliciano, the crew beamed to the surface.

The air felt heavy, damp, and humid to Gold, who shrugged his shoulders to adjust his uniform. Evora's sun shone bright and hot, seen here and there through some wispy cumulus clouds. Still, Gold smiled. His missions of late rarely allowed him to get planetside and he had trouble recalling the last time he had gotten a chance to be one of the first to visit a new world. The beam-down point was in a courtyard set before a low, massive building that had several archways decorated with sculptures of what the captain assumed to be native bird life. The birds had long wings, designed for maximum thrust, which made sense given the gravity.

Moments after the team materialized, one of the doors swung open and a delegation came out to greet them. Gold had seen pictures on screen but looked appraisingly at the Evorans. They were a short people, with none topping four and a half feet tall. He estimated they had a greater bone density and were possibly half again as heavy as an average human at that height. Each had dusky skin, with a large, two-lobed protrusion at the rear of the skull, mottled similar to Trill markings. Their ears were pinned against the sides of the head with large, triangular lobes. The Evorans were mainly covered in robes or gowns that were ornately decorated, the men more than the women. They wore head coverings that were not quite hats, not quite hoods.

"*Yew-cheen chef*-faw. I am Captain David Gold of the *U.S.S. da Vinci*," he said, stepping forward.

There was a brief moment as the delegation visibly winced and Gold realized he must have botched the greeting. In some cultures, that slight would have ended the meeting, started a war, or earned him a round of laughter. He was relieved to see that they simply avoided comment on the gaffe. The most decorated one of the group strode toward him, nodding her head in acknowledgment. "I am Vice-Regent Ilona," she said with a soft, melodic voice. "Regent Cuzar will join us in the conference chamber in a few minutes. Please follow me."

Ilona led the group through the main archway and into the building, which the captain guessed was a main government building. Inside, the walls were a light color, maybe beige, but hard to tell under harsh yellowish light. Every few feet there hung huge paintings of wildlife, none with people in them. The floors were a highly polished wood that reflected every boot click from the Starfleet personnel, filling the hallway with noise. The Evorans must have worn something soft-soled, since they moved noiselessly.

After a few turns, Ilona grasped two iron rings that hung on double doors and pulled. Silently, the doors opened and there was a room with a large round table within. A semicircular device was set in its center and the seating was a cushioned short-backed chair on wheels. Again, the walls were covered with drawings, paintings, and even holographic images of various fauna, set against the usual variety of natural environments.

Gold looked at the pictures and shot a questioning look to Abramowitz, who had been deeply studying everything with just her eyes. No doubt she wished she could use her tricorder, but she needed permission first. Abramowitz followed Gold's gaze to the walls and back again, and she just shrugged. He took that to mean his cultural specialist had no idea regarding the significance placed on the animals.

Ilona gestured, indicating the seats, and took her place at what looked to be her regular place. The others clustered around her, leaving one chair empty. Gold chose to take the chair directly opposite the open spot and winced as he tried to get comfortable in the wrongly proportioned seat. He chuckled to himself as the more massive Hawkins had an even tougher time sitting. On the other hand, Gomez and Abramowitz seemed to gracefully slide into their chairs.

Another Evoran entered the room, all by herself, and Gold studied her. She was older than the others, her eyes tired by his standards. Her outfit matched Ilona's in ornateness, which he took it to mean she was Cuzar, their regent. He liked that she was traveling without entourage or beefy security.

Unsure of the cultural protocol, he fell back on good Earth manners and rose, which prompted

the rest of his crew to stand as well. The seated
Evorans remained in their chairs, watching with
interest.

"*Yew-cheen chef*-faw, Regent." Once more there
were winces from behind the Regent, but she
seemed not to hear the mispronunciation. Gold
felt awful about the slight but kept silent. He had
to be better prepared next time he tried one of
these missions.

"Captain Gold, I am so glad to meet you," Cuzar
said, walking directly to him. Already, he liked her
for not reacting to the error. She held out a hand
with a smile on her face and Gold shook it, noting
its dry feel but firm grip. She was definitely older
than the others, with wrinkles and a pronounced
wattle under her chin. Her robe had a high collar
that rose to two points, framing the squarish face.
Gold made a quick round of introductions but
Cuzar did not reciprocate or even acknowledge
those seated around her table. "Thank you for
coming on such short notice." Unlike Ilona, her
voice showed its age and lacked any sense of
melody. It also sounded stressed.

"We're happy to help. Do you have more details
for us to work with?"

Cuzar rounded the table and took her seat, at
which point the Starfleet personnel also sat, with
Hawkins making an audible sound as he struggled
to be comfortable. "The device was left where it
was found but we do have additional graphics,"
the regent said. Reaching under the table, she
pressed something that activated the globe in the
table's center. At first it glowed softly, and then

above it emerged a hologram of a charred, cracked . . . something. Gold craned his neck for a look and noticed that Gomez was ducking hers to see underneath the item.

"Captain, this device predates our civilization by approximately fifty thousand years. At the time this was supposedly placed on the ground, Evora was filled with nothing but unevolved animal life—mostly reptiles and birds. It dates to a time when one entire species of animal life was mysteriously wiped out. Our scientists have been studying remains and geological evidence to better understand how our planet developed and how our species developed."

"What is it made of?" Gomez asked. Gold detected the unbridled curiosity in her voice.

"A metal compound totally unfamiliar to us," Cuzar replied. "It has an iron base, but there are other elements not currently found on our world."

"Then some alien life must have visited Evora," the engineer said.

Before Cuzar could reply, there were audible gasps from the previously silent Evorans. None looked at all pleased by the comment, especially one of the bulkier males. Gold noted that Cuzar slowly closed her eyes and breathed deeply for a moment.

"That's the conclusion Rugan, my chief archaeologist, also came up with," she said slowly. "Understand, Captain, all our religious beliefs hold that after several great cataclysms and cleansings, we were chosen to thrive and develop as a species . . . as a people. All previous life had been found wanting and removed to allow us to flourish. Never before had the notion been made that other intelligent life had been here before us. This has a great many people concerned and even fearful."

As she spoke, Gold glanced over toward Abramowitz, who was absorbed in the conversation but was also looking concerned. He could tell this was serious, as her eyebrows dropped and she barely blinked. This mission was getting more curious and more delicate by the moment.

"I don't want to be an alarmist," Gold began, hesitating to catch Cuzar's reaction. She blinked once but seemed ready for anything. "What would happen if we determined the artifact did come from a sentient race prior to the Evorans' evolution?"

The regent looked out at Gold, and scanned her retinue before commenting. Her eyes seemed to be searching for something. Finally, she regarded Gold and answered, "There are still some among my people who feel we have no business mixing with races not from Evora. They prefer things to be simple and as uncomplicated as possible. We have some religious sects that still do not believe we have truly left this world for the stars. Telling any of them that aliens had been here before us . . . it could create schisms that might lead to civil war."

Gold swallowed hard, his eyes glancing at Abramowitz, who nodded once. "Fear of the unknown is universal, Regent," he said slowly. "Fear of change is also widely known throughout the galaxy. Our training, though, makes us sensitive to those concerns and we will follow your lead. Now then, how would you like us to proceed?"

"I would like your people to go to the dig and examine it for yourself. Once you can tell me exactly what has been found, I will take *your* advice on how to proceed." She paused, looking at her own people. Her voice hardened as she concluded with, "Hiding this from my people, though, will not be an option."

Gold rose, nodding toward his crew. "Very good, Regent. I'll return to my ship and get out of the way. If you think I can do anything further to aid you, let me know."

Cuzar nodded toward him but did not rise. "Having you here is a boon, Captain Gold. I wish we had no need for you or your services but we must. Thank you again."

CHAPTER
3

A short time later, a small four-winged craft left the capitol building, taking the Starfleet crew to the site. Cuzar left the meeting chamber, her steps slow and measured. Security Provost Helanoman watched her with hatred burning in his eyes. Once the regent was out of sight, he turned to the others in the room.

"See? She *would* encourage more contamination from offworlders. Her search for this truth will bring curiosity seekers or fortune hunters or who knows what else. Evora will no longer be just our world but one we must share!"

"And what do you suggest the Onlith do?" This from Ilona, who remained in her seat, while Helanoman strode the room, his short red cape fluttering slightly in his wake. "She is our regent and we are pledged to follow her rule."

"The Onlith have opposed all contact beyond our solar system and that remains a perfectly attainable goal. There are enough people who share our beliefs that we hold almost a majority within the council. Our opinions need to be heeded. We have no desire to be visited or trade with others. Our planet is bountiful enough without foods or gems from distant races."

"And the technology they offer without price? Or their protection from others less benevolent?"

"Shira, you ask good questions but imagine our world at peace. We have nothing unique they want, we're not near any of their boundaries with hostile races. Evora can be left alone and that is as it should be."

The other woman, seated by Ilona, frowned. "What about the artifact? What if it tells them something that changes that?"

Helanoman whirled about, slamming an open hand atop the table, startling the four others in the room. "It cannot be true! If it is, then more will come and ruin our way! And that means the Federation must learn nothing. They will go away and we will exert our influence over Cuzar. I have people at the site and if it becomes necessary, the item will be destroyed."

"You would hide the truth?" Shira seemed very disturbed by the notion and Ilona was shaking her head in agreement.

"If this truth brings more contamination, then yes. Maybe we don't always need to know the truth."

"You think we can successfully defy the regent and her majority?"

"Shira, dear, the margin between them and us is under ten percent. If we can show how the

Federation ridicules our core beliefs, the numbers will change and *we* will be the majority. You'll see."

He also knew he had enough followers that his other plan would be launched at the same time. His fellow council members, already filled with doubt, would not stand in his way, but he was shrewd enough to know not to count on much support from them.

CHAPTER
4

Menali, a young Evoran male with one of the more brightly colored outfits Abramowitz had seen so far, was obviously enjoying playing tour guide. Every few moments, he would veer from one side of the narrow flitter to the other, excitedly describing natural and Evoran-made sites. His pride in the planet was clear and his smile infectious.

Next to her, Gomez proclaimed that the planet was a pretty one, and Abramowitz had to agree. The architecture emphasized shorter buildings, allowing for the distant mountains to act as backgrounds. She noted the cleanliness of the streets, towns, and waterways, leading her to believe they had long ago made land management a priority. When she asked, Menali breathlessly explained how the power plants were mostly thermodynamic and kept either underground or deep within mountain ranges with microwave technology beaming the energy to the farms, towns, and cities.

The cultural specialist made notes on everything he explained, planning to add it to the cultural database when the mission was complete.
She marveled that the Federation truly knew very
little of these people and their ways, yet felt secure
enough to make them a protectorate. She'd never
understand the Diplomatic Corps. "Regent Cuzar
seemed very concerned about the possibility of a
civil war. Have they been common on your
world?"

"*Seft*, no," he said. "Not this century, anyway.
We used to have a lot of them and they took their
toll. In *conitik* school we were taught that we
didn't reach the stars for so long because we were
so busy building weapons and defenses against
those weapons."

Abramowitz nodded sympathetically, interested
in how that might compare with the history of
other Federation worlds. "What made them finally
stop?"

"We finally built high-altitude fighters to intercept the missiles and some of the older pilots
formed a political party so they could show us once
and for all that we were just one people who needed
to look out for one another rather than fight."

To Abramowitz, that sounded too idealistic to
be true, but she also knew that that was how it
must have been taught in the schools. She'd have
to do further research to see the events in their
true context. That is, if the away team would be
granted access to such documentation.

"Menali," she asked, "are there histories I can
study to learn more?"

"Regent Cuzar announced recently that we're going to improve our libraries. I guess we weren't very good record keepers during all those fights," he said with a shrug.

Gomez shot her a questioning look and Abramowitz tilted her head and narrowed her eyes. It would make their studies and research harder, the gesture told the first officer. Whatever this mission promised, it would be more complicated to achieve. Gomez returned a look that was intended to say, *When ever are these missions easy?*

In his security alcove, Helanoman sat at the huge semicircular master station and signaled several of his colleagues, positioned throughout the city. All the signal contained was a time. Within seconds, each recipient signaled back with a single word: *ready.*

He then turned his attention to the worldnet and its observations of the *da Vinci* far overhead. Captain Gold seemed like a veteran, albeit soft, used to ferrying these engineers around. He showed Cuzar more sympathy than mettle— but Helanoman also knew of Starfleet's reputation. When the Onlith acted, they would have to do so in such a way that Gold and his ship would not be involved. Indeed, when they took control of the government, Helanoman would simply send the ship away and they would leave out of deference to the wishes of the new administration.

His administration.

* * *

The flitter landed in a cloud of dust that was quickly dispersed in the hot air. It was a smooth ride, Gomez admitted to herself, and she did like the opportunity to see the world rather than just transport to the archaeological site. Sometimes the old-fashioned ways were still good ones. Menali certainly provided them with a great deal of information, although much of it seemed more interesting than useful. Still, one never knew. Her experiences with the S.C.E. proved that time after time.

Four people approached the craft with one clearly the senior leader. Menali said this would be Cuzar's chief scientist, Rugan. She seemed much older than the others, so Gomez asked Menali about her.

"Rugan lives and breathes research," he explained. "She's just over fifty and most of our people are retired by then, doing spiritual service and the like. Rugan, they say, will never give up and will be entombed with her microscope."

Abramowitz looked up at that and asked, "How long do your people live, Menali?"

"Our oldest living person is sixty-three, and he claims it's the high altitudes of his mountain home."

Abramowitz turned to Gomez and commented, "I'd like to know if their short life span is natural or a result of all their wars."

"That's not why we're here, you know," Gomez said.

"I know," she said with a sigh. "I wish we could get Elizabeth down here to give them an exam."

Gomez shook her head. "Menali notwithstanding, they seem so private that I suspect that would never happen. But now that you mention it, the captain was asking me about Elizabeth this morning. She seem okay to you?" Abramowitz and the doctor were not especially close friends, Gomez knew, but the captain's question had been on her mind.

"I guess so. Why?"

"Never mind." The flitter's doors opened and Menali led the officers onto the sun-hardened surface. He made the introductions and Rugan smiled briefly at each one, but Gomez suspected she'd rather be digging than making nice to a bunch of people from Starfleet. Still, they were here to help and she was beginning to get fidgety herself.

"The item is this way," Rugan said in a rough voice, and abruptly turned, expecting everyone to follow at her pace. While she had shorter legs than the officers, the planet's higher gravity slowed them down, so keeping pace was more involved than Gomez expected. As they walked, she saw tents, some prefab constructs, and lighting equipment, little different from what she had seen on a dozen other worlds. No doubt Rugan drove them day and night.

After five minutes, they arrived at an area that had been opened like an incision, long and deep but not especially wide. The sides of the dig were smooth with mounds of sifted, light tan dirt lining the dig. No one was working within the hole at the moment, although Gomez saw several varieties of insect life-forms, all slimy, long-legged, and with pincers. Several were crawling atop the reason for their visit.

The item looked like a round, fat blob. It was a dusty uniform purple color and connected to piping that vanished within the crust. There were bulbous protrusions all around the object that seemed to be controls of some sort.

Gomez took out her tricorder and began scanning the item from above. The readings were coming back as a metallic compound, matching what the Evorans had already told the crew. The age estimate also seemed to match. However, her more sophisticated tricorder could also tell that there was still some form of power running through the object, low-level but steady.

She crouched for a better look, ignoring those around her. In fact, if anyone was talking, she didn't notice, fascinated as she was by the item. Its design defied identification and if that was a language scrawled on the sides of the pipes it was not at all one she or the tricorder could identify. After a moment she stopped to wipe sweat from her forehead and realized she was genuinely excited by this prospect. It didn't seem to be threatening—and she knew from threatening alien technology.

"Carol, this thing is amazing," she finally said, standing and brushing herself off. "It's everything Cuzar told us it would be and more. It's obviously connected to something else and I think it's still active."

Rugan hurried over, an unhappy look on her

lined face. "What do you mean, still active? What is it?"

"Clearly it's old. Beyond that, I don't know yet," Gomez admitted. "And I think that's writing on the pipes. Do you recognize it?"

"It's not remotely like any Evoran writing I've ever studied," she said with distaste.

Gomez tapped her communicator. "Gomez to *da Vinci*. Captain, we're at the site and sure enough, that thing doesn't seem to belong to the Evora. There's some writing on it we can't place. Can you spare Bart for the mission?"

"I think we can," Gold said, a touch of amusement in his voice. *"Anything else you've seen?"*

"We've only been here a little while, but no. Carol has been talking to their chief scientist, Rugan, and Hawkins, well, he's looking a little lost and bored."

"If it's all the same, I want to leave him with you and Abramowitz."

"No problem with me. Gomez out." She turned to Vance, who did indeed look out of place and restless. "Sorry, Hawkins, but you've got to keep me safe."

"I can handle it," he said with a smile. "Might be the first time I hit planetside without winding up in sickbay."

"Rugan," Carol said, returning their attention to the dig. "Have you considered widening this stretch to see where these pipes lead?"

"No, Dr. Abramowitz," she said unhappily. "Once we cleared this off and realized what it was, no one wanted much to do with it. Many of these locals we use are strictly religious and they don't know what to do with this new information."

"Well," Gomez said, "to better understand this, we need it widened. If there's another of these . . . nodes . . . we should try and find it."

Rugan tugged at her chin with a wrinkled hand. "Wouldn't digging risk damaging it? If there's power running through it, that could be trouble."

Abramowitz hadn't considered that aspect and she shot a quick glance at Gomez. The first officer shrugged, uncertain herself at this point. Abramowitz turned back to the wizened scientist.

"Without digging further, we might never figure out what you've found. Starfleet is good, but even we need more to work with."

The scientist nodded and turned to talk to several of the nearby laborers.

"Feliciano to Gomez."

Surprised to be hearing from the transporter chief, Gomez tapped her combadge. "Go ahead, Diego."

"Commander, I can't beam Mr. Faulwell directly into the dig site. There's some kind of interference. I also don't have a positive lock on the away team."

Gomez took out her tricorder. "The power emissions from the item must be interfering with the transporter. Beam him down as close as you can."

"Acknowledged."

Seconds later, Bart Faulwell materialized about twenty-five meters from where they stood, unnoticed by all save Gomez and Hawkins. He apparently had been paying attention to the reports and tricorder readings, because in addition to his own equipment, he was wearing a bright blue hat.

"Over here, Bart," Gomez called. He ambled over, smiling and nodding at the locals but keeping his distance. Once he joined Gomez and Abramowitz, he leaned over the hole and stared at the item. She laughed when he made a face at its odd shape but she also noticed that his eyes went right to the writing and his lips began moving.

"I was checking the database and this doesn't seem to match any of the races that we know were in this sector one hundred thousand years back," Faulwell noted. Gomez appreciated his preparation even though he was not slated to be part of the away team. Still, it made sense that he might be needed and no doubt he knew it.

"Carol, is there anything you've learned that I should know about?"

"Not yet," she said, coming closer and leaning over the edge. "You'll have to crack this one without a clue."

"Swell."

"Hey," Abramowitz said, "you're the one who says you like challenges."

Faulwell smiled. "Good point . . ."

CHAPTER
5

The time had come. Flanked by three heavily armored followers, Helanoman walked with purpose down the stretch of corridor connecting his security alcove to Cuzar's private office. As head of security, he certainly knew of any escape routes and had people posted at all five exits.

A glance at his tactical gauntlet told the Onlith leader that his people were also positioned by the public entrances and exits with still more by the vehicle bay. He had planned long and hard for the moment, drilling his most faithful followers, all waiting for the signal to assemble and reclaim the government for the Evoran people.

Helanoman didn't necessarily dislike the off-worlders he had met, but they had nothing to contribute to his way of life. He did see, though, the contamination they would bring with them and the changes to the orderly, peaceful, and spiritual life they led. Nothing in his religious studies had prepared him to accept signs of life other than that which naturally occurred on his homeworld.

With a silent gesture, he positioned the followers to protect the entrance, letting him enter the office alone.

The door opened silently and he could see Cuzar at her writing table, stylus in hand, otherwise alone. Monitors behind her showed a parade of news digests, fed to the regent's office from around the globe. There was more than enough to occupy a planetary leader around the clock.

Cuzar looked up and saw the security officer, and her eyes had a glint of recognition. She remained still, unmoving. "So," she said softly, "this is the way it is to be?"

"The Onlith have warned you and the government often enough." Helanoman entered the office. He looked around, mentally rearranging the furniture to a pattern more his style.

"Your party has seats in the council. We hear you and have acted with respect to your beliefs. Why this way?"

"Because of what you found," he answered. "Because of the ship in orbit. Everything we warned you about is coming to pass." He walked to the desk, trying to loom over Cuzar and intimidate her, but she remained still. With a short bark, he summoned one of his followers, who systematically searched the room for weapons. Finding none, he was sent back out of the office. Cuzar sat motionlessly the entire time.

"What now, Helanoman? Public beheading? Bloodletting?"

He smiled coldly. "Nothing of the sort, Regent. We want this to be orderly and will do nothing to turn you into a martyr to rally your own followers. Instead, you and I shall stay here while the Onlith take possession of the media. We have already seized the travel centers so no one can come to your aid. Evora will be at peace once again."

An hour after the crew began digging, enough dirt had been cleared away to expose a three-meter stretch of the pipe. Abramowitz and Gomez used their tricorders to further examine the alien artifact, but neither one seemed to learn anything new. There were, though, more of the alien characters, which excited Faulwell. Gomez sighed and stepped back, letting the eager linguist study at length.

As Faulwell did his work, Rugan came up to Gomez and asked about progress. She had a look in her eyes not dissimilar to the one Bart had, which intrigued Sonya.

"There's some organic residue on one stretch of the pipe and we'd need to take actual scrapings to better learn from it, but my initial readings confirm it is not native to Evora. Since you don't recognize the writing, everything leads to the conclusion that whatever this was came from another culture."

Careful as she was to modulate her voice to sound sympathetic, Gomez was afraid of a negative reaction. Instead, Rugan kept looking at her with interest, expecting her to continue.

"You're taking this better than I expected," Gomez added with a grin.

"My dear, I am a scientist first and always," she said, her voice strong. "Once we learned there were other races among the stars, I began wondering about our own little world. Had we been visited? I admit, it's not a popular thought, but it has been the stuff of our fiction lately."

"Will this really bring about civil war as the regent fears?" This from Abramowitz, who wandered closer.

"Maybe," the scientist answered. "I hope not, but so much has been discovered in just this generation. I hope I live another decade or two to see what else we can find, but I doubt that will happen. These old bones are already wearing down."

Gomez smiled kindly. "You seem one-of-a-kind."

Rugan nodded, her timeworn face showing concern. "Would that I were not."

With their attention directed toward the dig, none of the Starfleet personnel noticed that several of the local workers and some of the science staff had been moving away. They had been backing up toward the tents.

Hawkins caught some movement from his left side and whirled in time to see three people emerge, carrying weapons that were strapped to their arms. He reached for his own phaser, moving toward the people and away from his colleagues. One raised the weapon, clearly some energy-discharging gun, and took aim. Crying a warning to the others, Hawkins leapt to his right and fired off a quick burst. The shot went wide, but so did the one from the Evoran weapon.

The sound of weapons being fired alerted everyone and there was a scramble to find protective cover. Gomez swore out loud at not being armed, but there had been nothing to lead her to believe that anyone but Hawkins would need a phaser. Now she regretted the act and crawled to get behind one of the dirt mounds. It would offer scant protection, she knew, but it was better than nothing until she could assess the situation. Abramowitz had leapt into the dig, seeking cover with Faulwell, while Rugan merely ran to the dig.

Quickly, Gomez scanned the area and determined that they were outgunned and outnumbered. They were also pinned down here in the dig site; the *da Vinci* wouldn't be able to beam them out this close to the item. For now, at least, they had to stay put and see how this played out. At least she could notify Captain Gold, and she tapped her combadge. Briefly, she told the captain what was happening and kept the channel open.

Hawkins had managed to keep up a barrage of fire that disoriented the clearly untrained Evorans. He worked his way to Gomez, trying to provide protection while waiting for orders.

Before she could give any, though, one of the scientists managed to come up from behind and hurl a huge rock at Gomez, stunning her. As Hawkins turned to fire, three weapons discharged and two beams struck him, rendering him unconscious. With the lone defensive weapon silent, the Evorans swarmed over the area, with several pointing their weapons into the dig site, keeping Abramowitz and Faulwell trapped.

The Onlith were now successful both at the capitol and at the archaeological site.

CHAPTER
6

"Gomez!" Gold repeated the commander's name several more times before giving up. Clearly, his crew was in trouble, trapped by hostile forces.

Kieran Duffy stood silently beside the captain, lending moral support since there didn't seem to be much more he could do. McAllan was already running scans of the planet, while Ina was checking the planet's broadcast signals. Gold began pacing the small bridge, unhappy that he could merely stand around. He had done it often enough to accept it, never to like it. Unfortunately, it was all they could do for the moment. The best tactical option—beaming them out—wasn't available as long as the away team was still in the dig site.

"Captain," Ina called from her ops station, "I'm picking up a series of media reports from all continents. It sounds like we're being accused of some form of alien contamination. They sound angry about it, not scared."

Gold began a reply before McAllan spoke up.

"All weapons fire has stopped," the tactical officer reported.

"That's something," Gold said. "Life signs?"

"All present and accounted for," McAllan crisply
replied. "But the placement of the away team's
combadges doesn't match the location of the
four human life signs. They've probably been removed."

"Not surprising. Get me Regent Cuzar."

McAllan nodded once and began tapping at his
controls. After a few moments he looked at the
captain and said, "No response from the capitol.
We're getting through but they're choosing not to
answer."

Gold paced some more, this time joined by
Corsi, who had just arrived on the bridge. She kept
pace while asking for an update. Once Gold finished, she asked, "Shall I assemble an assault
team?"

The captain slowly shook his head. "Not until
we know something for certain. There are too
many unknowns for us to risk more crew."

"Our reports indicate they have several star-
worthy craft. We can outfly and outgun them, but
can they outnumber us?"

Duffy shook his head. "All scans show there are
no hidden starships or additional weapons
depots."

Gold added, "Cuzar has been scrupulously honest with us since we arrived. This is something
way beyond her control."

Corsi looked at Gold with a penetrating stare,

one she usually used on interrogation subjects. "Then who's in control down there?"

"I wish we knew."

Gomez groaned as she rolled onto to her right side. Whatever was thrown at her clearly damaged a rib or two. Once she figured this situation out, someone was going to pay. First the monster shii tore open her torso on Sarindar, then the monster "Nat" had cracked a couple of ribs on Maeglin, now this.

First things first, though; she was in command of the away team and needed to assess the situation. Opening her eyes to slits, she looked about without moving her head more than a degree or two at a time. The armed Evorans had a small group of fellow citizens sitting in a small cluster near a storage unit. Guards were posted between her position and the dig. Abramowitz and Faulwell had been brought up to the surface and were seated by the still unconscious Hawkins, who of course did not have his phaser. None of them had their combadges, either. Interestingly, Rugan was seated between her and her fellow *da Vinci* crewmates.

"What's going on?" she croaked through dry lips.

Rugan leaned over, passing along a small bottle of water. Gomez wet her lips, which hurt from the sun, and took several small swallows. The cool water made her feel better and she began to slowly sit up. She smiled at the relieved looks on her crewmates' faces.

"I knew the Onlith were serious about avoiding cross-cultural contact," the scientist said sympathetically. "I just never knew they would act like this, like barbarians."

"Who . . . are the Onlith?"

"A faction that has wedged its way into our government. They've opposed every step we've taken off this world, which is why we have not been better neighbors. The Onlith have been very persuasive to our masses, indicating that our every way of life was going to be irrevocably changed if the Federation—or worse, some of the other races we've encountered—came to stay."

Gomez nodded, having heard such fears before. With each passing minute, her head felt better and she was thinking more clearly. Not that this meant any immediate plans came to mind, but at least she was alert.

"I know your people have preached how you respect the way of life for each world," Rugan continued. "I saw that when I toured your *Enterprise*. But it's hard to communicate that to three hundred million people, a good number of whom are scared to death of change. Me, I always want to know the truth, to understand our place in the galaxy."

The two sat in companionable silence for several minutes, just looking out at the Onlith followers. During that time, Hawkins roused and was allowed some water by a guard. He was slow to sit up but once he did, he winked at Gomez, so she was glad he was not concussed once more. One of the Onlith seemed to be in communication with a leader elsewhere, and when the conversation ended, she signaled to three people by the storage unit.

In short order, several small devices were removed and carried toward the dig. Gomez watched as Rugan stiffened and let out a small cry. "No, no, please don't . . ." she whispered, but received no reply.

"Are they going to . . . ?"

"Yes, my dear, they want to destroy that which they do not understand."

Two guards gestured to the Starfleet crew and the Evoran scientist to move away, forcing them back several meters. Keeping their weapons trained on them, the guards seemed to be fearful of what was about to happen behind them, but Gomez saw no way to exploit that. She would have to continue to wait for time and opportunity. Gold, she imagined, was doing the same from orbit.

There was a muffled sound as the devices exploded, showering the area with clouds of dirt that hung in the hot, still air. Although the device had been destroyed, Gomez knew that the pipes underneath the ground were intact beyond the dig, which meant the alien presence continued on Evora. She wondered if these Onlith would try and remove that evidence of previous contact, as well.

"Sir, there's been an explosion at the dig," Ina called out, her voice high and excited.

Duffy was peering over the operations officer's

shoulder. "It seems localized, at the exact spot where the artifact was located."

"All life signs accounted for," Ina added.

Gold sighed with relief. "Destroy what you do not understand," he muttered, understanding the nameless fear that seemed to grip a world.

"Message from the capitol, sir," McAllan said quickly.

Standing up, Gold turned to face the viewscreen and nodded once for contact to be established. He was not overly surprised to recognize one of the people from the meeting chamber. In fact, he was more than a little disappointed to see it was the head of the security forces. To Gold, it was too predictable, and it made a sick sort of sense to him.

"Captain Gold, I wish to inform you of a change in government here on Evora."

"A *coup d'état?* Why am I not surprised?"

Helanoman blinked as he tried to comprehend the French phrase but it was not translating properly. *"You expected this?"*

"Fear has led to rash actions more times than I can count," the captain replied, trying to keep things conversational and not confrontational. If this was to be the new leader, he had to tread delicately. "My people. Are they unharmed? And your regent?"

"Your crew are fine although in my custody, as is Cuzar."

"What next? Try her for crimes against the people?"

The Onlith leader shook his head. *"She did what*

she thought was best for the people. The people think otherwise."

"So you know what the people want better than Cuzar does? How so?"

"We listen to them, Captain. We hear them in the schools, in the workplace, in the home. She is so enthralled by the life among the stars, she is deaf to her own kind. I hear all and have acted to preserve our way of life."

Gold whirled back to the screen. "And that includes obfuscating the truth?"

"I did what needed doing and will continue to act in the interests of Evora," Helanoman said. His expression grew colder. *"Pledge the Federation will leave Evora alone and not return. Do so, and I will release your people."*

"You realize that I do not act entirely on my own. I must consult with Starfleet Command and they must speak with the Federation Council. This may take some time."

The Evoran looked appraisingly at the captain and Gold knew the man was shrewd. He was weighing the facts, imagining how he would act were their positions reversed. Was Gold merely stalling or was he truly unable to commit on behalf of the United Federation of Planets? Meantime, Gold took the pause in dialogue to look around the bridge. P8 Blue had arrived, and was looking at him intently. She clearly had something to share.

"Either way, Helanoman, I need time, as I suspect you do, too. Arrange to bring my people to the capitol while I speak with my government. Gold out."

No sooner did the screen switch back to the planet beneath the starship than the captain began giving orders. "McAllan, send that conversation and my last three log entries to Starfleet. Send a separate signal to the Federation Council."

"Same message?"

"It doesn't matter," Gold said tersely. "We just have to look like we're holding up our end of the deal. Blue, what did you find?"

The insectoid engineer said, "Sir, their equipment checks out as significantly inferior to ours. They may not be able to track our signals or even tap into them to verify the content. And, they may not be geared to scan for transporter activity."

Gold nodded and looked at Duffy and Corsi. "Good. Let's make plans."

Gomez managed to move over to where the others sat. Hawkins had regained his alertness and was watching the area with keen interest. Abramowitz was trailing fingers in the dirt and Faulwell seemed to just sit and stare.

"You okay, Bart?"

"You never expect it, do you?"

"What do you mean?"

"Violence. Destruction."

She thought about it a moment and then realized he was in danger just hours after his partner was in a similar situation across the quadrant. "It's always been a part of the package," she said gently. "We take the oath knowing we might face such dangers. Our lives are on the line every time we undertake a mission. It's no different at a starbase."

"I understand that, Commander, but it seemed to rattle Anthony more than I've ever seen before."

"Didn't you two meet during the war?" Abramowitz asked.

"Yeah, when I was doing crypto work on Starbase 92. But that wasn't exactly the front lines. Anyhow, I have some leave time coming, and I was hoping I could visit him to help . . . but now I'm stuck here with a bunch of fanatics."

"This? This is nothing, Bart. I've faced down the Borg, Captain Gold fought back a Romulan incursion once, and heck, McAllan nearly lost everything during the Proxima Beta incident."

Faulwell snorted derisively at the incidents, since after all, that was then, and now, well, now things did look a little less than wonderful. "He needs me, Sonya."

"I'm sure he does, Bart," she said sympathetically. "And you will be there for him. And if not, then it's because you were doing your duty. Look at Soloman and how well he has adjusted to losing his life partner. We're survivors. And we're fighters. I have no intention of sitting here until the Onlith decide to make examples of us, or put us on trial or whatever stupid thing they think of. Right now, put Anthony out of your mind and let me figure out the next step. We won't be idle for long."

Faulwell thought a moment and with a slight smile added, "Thank you."

"Don't mention it," she replied, and turned her attention to the movements of the Onlith guards.

Bart sat silent for a few more moments. While she felt for him, Gomez certainly didn't want him distracted when she needed everyone focused on their current predicament.

"Look, if I'm going to have to sit here, can I at least use my tricorder?"

Gomez watched with interest to see how the Evorans guarding them reacted to Faulwell's request. The dirt had settled a few minutes ago, coating everything with a thin film of brown. Whatever that item had been, it was now gone for good.

The three Evorans exchanged blank expressions and shrugs. Finally, the one closest to the linguist nodded and then settled in a chair to watch. Faulwell looked over to Gomez and shrugged also, then turned to his tricorder. He must have carefully recorded all the alien writing on the artifact and was looking it over.

Gomez looked around the area, figuring there might be an opportunity coming, especially if one of the guards was paying close attention to one of them. She continued to watch each Evoran, wondering if the trapped workers would fight alongside her if she broke free. She couldn't begin to guess and it was then she missed having Corsi around for help. While Gomez could diagnose and fix just about any mechanical problem, tactics were not her strong suit. With a wry smile to herself, she realized that, after her chat with Faulwell, she might, at least, make a halfway decent counselor.

She continued to consider options but found it troubling to concentrate now that she noticed Faulwell humming quite contentedly to himself.

At least one member of the crew was able to work on the original mission.

Abramowitz was also looking over Faulwell's shoulder, nodding every now and then. Then her expression changed: her eyes went wide, her head cocked to one side, and her expression was one of revelation.

"Bart, that humming, it's reminding me of something. I need to check in with the *da Vinci*."

"Fat chance," Faulwell said with a smirk. "What do you recall?"

Before she could reply, there was a low rumble that built quickly into a full-scale tremor. The Evorans seemed especially surprised and looked from one to another for guidance. As it rapidly built in intensity, Gomez determined that there'd never be a better time for action.

"Vance, now!" was all she managed to say before tumbling to her knees and then rolling to her sore side. The earthquake was causing everyone to fall, and it was intense enough to bring down the storage units. She could hear the cries from scared or injured people.

Still, she hoped it would end and was determined to have the upper hand when that happened. Struggling to her knees, despite the heavy gravity, she saw that Hawkins, better trained in these circumstances, was already wrestling with a guard to grab her weapon. He kicked twice, stunning the smaller Evoran, and ripped the weapon from the straps to her arm. Hawkins hefted it in both hands and shoulder-rolled to avoid two charging Evorans.

"Find the combadges!" Gomez yelled. She struggled to her feet, noticing the quake was beginning to subside.

"Where did that come from?" demanded Gold.

McAllan and Ina were feverishly working their stations, checking incoming data. "It's registering 6.5 on the Richter scale, localized to a nine-square-kilometer range," McAllan called out.

"Media reports sound panicked," Ina added. "It's like they've never seen one before."

"Scan the planet. Are there any other incidents? Then scan deep, I want a geologic picture of this place." He'd be damned if he was going to respect protocol when his people and possibly the planet's population were threatened.

His people worked quickly but it was not fast enough for the captain, who remained frustrated that his away team was out of touch and that a fanatic seemed to be controlling the planet. But he was not entirely helpless. He looked over his shoulder and nodded at Corsi, who returned the gesture and turned for the turbolift.

As soon as she was gone, he signaled below. "Soloman, get cracking on the transmitted tricorder readings. See what you can learn." As the Bynar acknowledged the instruction, Gold got restless with the waiting.

CHAPTER
7

"Why aren't you doing something?"

Cuzar looked at Helanoman with unconcealed contempt. She always feared some loss of power, but had hoped it was through democratic means, not a coup. Her desktop screens flashed with information showing the devastating results of the earthquake. In all her life, she had never experienced one, never had to govern through one—she knew of the term only from the cultural information exchange they had had with the Federation.

The man who would be her successor looked equally inexperienced. And Cuzar was sure that he had not availed himself of the Federation database that would have at least given him a name for the phenomenon that racked their world.

"I can't stop the planet from shaking," he shouted at her. "What would you have me do?"

"Help the people," she said quietly, refusing to let her emotions escalate this into a screaming match. "Dispatch your troops to render aid, fly out medics, see what supplies are needed. If we've lost power, as I fear, you'll need engineers."

"I should risk more lives?" He seemed out of his element, capable of fighting wars but not governing, and this, strangely, brought her a sense of satisfaction.

"It's over," she pointed out. "Go help the people you are trying to preserve from alien contamination."

Helanoman glared at her and then removed his portable communications device from the ornate belt he wore. Quickly, he barked orders that were almost word for word what the regent had suggested. She smiled but remained still at the desk, studying the telemetry reports. A flashing light to her left caught her attention.

"The *da Vinci* is trying to make contact."

"Ignore them," the security officer demanded.

"Hard to negotiate with them when you won't talk to them." She folded her hands and watched him, feeling more serene by the moment.

"I have a planetary crisis to tend to, the Federation can wait." He paced a bit, barked some more orders to his troops, and then walked behind Cuzar, and she instinctively flinched. He chuckled mirthlessly and leaned over her right shoulder, looking at the screens. His fingers tapped with nervous energy against the desktop, and although this was annoying, it quietly pleased the woman. If he wanted to run a planet, so be it. *There's more to it than private rooms and having people curry favor. He'll learn,* she thought.

Her thoughts darkened. *But will he learn before another quake occurs?*

Instantaneous was not fast enough for Corsi. She desperately wanted to free her colleagues and get them off the planet. Bad enough a coup broke out, but severe tremors were another thing. People she could beat; entire planets were something else. Even for her.

The transporter beam released her and the phaser rifle was already swiveling back and forth, seeking the first target. Corsi took aim at three figures near her colleagues, thumbed an adjustment to widen the beam, and then pulled the trigger. The bright amber beam was filtered through the dust still hanging thickly in the air and it looked odd to the security chief.

As the figures dropped, she waved to Gomez and then pivoted to her right, taking aim at approaching Onlith followers. Two quick shots dropped the nearest attackers and she grunted in disbelief at how poorly armed they were.

"Where's Hawkins?" she shouted above the noise.

"Behind you," he replied, strolling with a big grin on his face and his left arm cradling the combadges, his own phaser gripped in his right hand.

"Status," she demanded.

"You stunned the last of the followers. No one is seriously hurt although they did manage to destroy the artifact before Commander Gomez could suss it out."

Corsi looked at Hawkins and was surprised by

how calm he seemed, and how in control of the situation he was. No doubt, had she not beamed down, he would have been able to take out the poorer-trained threat. "So, are you saying you didn't need any help?"

"Not especially, but it's awfully nice to have you here," he said, still smiling. When he saw her we-are-not-amused expression, the corners of his mouth dropped.

"If it's all the same to you, I'll remain here just in case."

"Wouldn't want it any other way, Commander."

The two walked to where Gomez, Abramowitz, and Faulwell were dusting themselves off. Corsi thought it a futile gesture given how much dust lingered in the air. She didn't bother, although she cradled the rifle so as to minimize contact with the air.

"Is anyone seriously hurt?" she asked to be safe.

"Scrapes, but nothing that requires Dr. Lense," Gomez replied.

Faulwell turned to Abramowitz and asked, "Now where were we?"

"Your humming," she said.

"His humming?" Corsi asked, wondering what kind of work was being done.

"Tone Deaf over here was humming as he reviewed the scans of the artifact. The sound, while annoying at first, got me to thinking. If we can't match the symbols to letters, it might be tones."

Faulwell snapped his fingers and brightened. "Sure, several known languages are musical, not verbal as we know it. In fact, certain regions of the galaxy have more language written in musical scales than in cuneiform. Why didn't I see that?"

"Perhaps the Onlith holding weapons on us?" Gomez offered.

"Or the earthquake," Hawkins suggested.

"My friends," Faulwell said with a combined snarl and grin. Quickly, he reopened his tricorder and called up the images he had been studying. Corsi, just mildly curious, peered over a shoulder to see what the artifact had looked like.

"Damnedest notes I've ever seen," she muttered.

"That's because they weren't written by Earth composers," Faulwell said absently. He hummed various notes, thumbing his tricorder to begin recording his voice. The pitch rose and fell and in a short time, Corsi came to a conclusion.

Faulwell was indeed tone-deaf.

She gestured for Hawkins to follow her, and together they began moving the still stunned Onlith bodies into one place. One of the Evorans offered to help, but given the size difference, Corsi shook him off.

"Stay here and keep an eye on them," she ordered Hawkins.

"I don't think they're smart enough to try again, but one never knows with fanatics," he said.

"Is that what they are?"

"The Onlith seem to believe the planet's destiny is to stay isolated," he explained. "So they mounted a coup and forced the planet to cut ties with the Federation. They won't even consider the alien nature of that doohickey."

Corsi nodded and Hawkins seemed glad she didn't ask any follow-up questions. Without knowing more about the artifact or the details of the coup, they were all uncomfortable with the situation. It remained too volatile for Corsi's liking and she couldn't figure out the best way to be prepared for what might come next. All of her training told her to be ready, to stay several steps ahead of her opponent and to know the opponent as well as he knows himself. In this case, she could not do either and it grated against her.

P8 Blue was using the sensors at one of their most powerful settings to study the spot where her colleagues were. Rarely had she needed to so often refine the controls, adjusting the sensors to screen out anomalous elements. It was slow-going work, learning a planet's geology at the same time as tracing the exact nature of the unearthed piping.

It was important work, and she liked being able to make a contribution to the mission, but still she disliked the pace.

However, several hours after starting the scans, the Nasat thought she had enough information to make a proper report to the captain. Gold had not allowed himself to sleep, but had taken a few minutes to retrieve some food from the mess. No sooner had he entered the bridge, causing McAllan to dutifully call out his presence, than Blue gestured to get his attention.

"What do you have, Blue?" He was holding a plate full of fruit in one hand and a glass of something dark in the other. The fruit was ripe and fresh, and the very smell of it almost made Blue ill, but she managed to control her reaction.

"Sir, the pipe work Commander Gomez found seems to be part of a network. From what I can tell, it extends under the entire planet."

Gold put down his plate and studied the schematic on the screen closest to the science station the Nasat was using. "Are you saying it's under every continent and ocean?"

"Yes. The metallurgical analysis is incomplete but I have to agree that it is not of Evoran origin."

The two studied the slowly revolving image of the planet and saw the complete network, like an ill-shaped spider's web, ring the world. Gold asked about the slowly changing colors of the web.

"It seems the network is giving off a very steady form of low-level harmonic vibrations. The color shift shows the change in frequency."

"What are the harmonics' purpose?" Gold took a bite from the banana and continued to stare at the screen.

"Captain, there are nodes like the one the away team was examining throughout Evora. They seem to be located where the tectonic plates meet or overlap. This entire network seems designed to prevent earthquakes from occurring."

"And when the Onlith destroyed the node, the next thing you had there was an earthquake."

Blue nodded vigorously and added, "With one node out of commission, the others are trying to compensate, hence the change in frequency."

"Keep checking the plates," Gold ordered.

"Figure out if the node needs to be replaced and if not, what happens next."

"Yes, sir," Blue said, chiming with her dedication. "My geology's a bit rusty, but I should be able to figure it out."

"How long have you been up here without a break? Maybe you should have some food—that's always good for the soul."

Chiming with amusement, Blue said, "I'd better not, sir. Remember what happened the last time I ate on the bridge?"

Gold wrinkled his nose, which indicated to Blue that he did remember. Humans had such sensitive olfactory senses—couldn't even bear a small rotting *greela*. Since that unfortunate incident, after which half the bridge crew grew ill, she ate by herself.

She turned back to the problem at hand, while Gold took his fruit back to the command chair.

Five minutes after he settled in his chair after getting Blue's report, Gold got a signal from the capitol. Helanoman's unpleasant visage graced the main viewer shortly thereafter.

"What does your Federation have to say?"

Well, he wasn't wasting any time. The man looked more intense than usual, and maybe a little stressed.

"First, how is the regent?"

"Unharmed. Now tell me."

"Second, you do know there was an earthquake on your world."

"Of course I know that."

"Do you require assistance?"

"Not from you! For all I know, it was your people that triggered the tremor to spread fear and dissent."

"I doubt you needed any help from us to do that."

The mild rebuke startled the Evoran for a moment but he quickly recovered, resuming his bluster. *"Maybe it was the artifact that caused the problem. Uninvited alien interference that could bring about our own destruction."*

"Want to hear another interpretation?"

"Not from you."

"Very well. No, I have not heard back from my government." Gold was beginning to enjoying playing with the man, clearly out of his element as a planetary leader. He could only imagine what Cuzar thought listening to this buffoon.

"You may still leave."

"Not before we see to it your world is spared further trouble."

"What do you mean?"

"You didn't want to hear it before."

"Hear what?"

Oh, this was getting too easy for the captain. "The truth."

"And I am to believe this truth?"

"Truth is truth, Helanoman," Gold said, taking on the tone of a teacher. "The sun rises in the morning. That is the truth. Your very world is in grave danger. That too is the truth."

Helanoman let out a guttural noise and cut the signal.

Gold leaned back and smiled. He knew the

Evoran would be calling back, but he hoped it was before the planet was in more trouble.

Blue stepped forward. "Sir, left alone, that network would have kept working, untouched by anyone. However, destroying the node has exposed the system's age—it cannot compensate to prevent another quake."

"Is one building up?"

"The aftershocks of the first quake will begin any moment," she said sadly.

"They'll be bad, eh?"

"Yes, sir, and I suspect numerous. The planet has not been allowed to naturally adjust itself for millennia. It may be just getting started."

"And if we replace the node?"

"We put the world back to sleep."

Without hesitation, he signaled Gomez and briefed her. As tersely as possible, Gold covered the situation and finished with, "You may have as little as thirty minutes before the aftershocks. Are you free to work?"

"Hawkins is watching the troublemakers," his first officer replied. *"Have Pattie send me her research and I'll tell you what supplies will be needed. Better start with a portable replicator so I can make my own magic."*

"Good luck, Gomez," Gold said gravely.

"You know what he was trying to tell you," Cuzar said.

"What? That aliens shoved their technology under the ground to save us?"

"Something like that, yes," she replied. She

needed to stay calm to avoid inciting him further. He wasn't stupid, she knew, but already she could tell that the strain was getting to him, because if Gold's truth was accurate, then the core beliefs Helanoman held were being shaken. Perhaps worse than the quake.

"Everything was fine until the starship arrived," he said, more to himself than anyone.

"Not really, and you know it," she said. "They arrived because of what we found. It was here first."

"Not before us!" he yelled and clenched his hands, trembling to avoid striking her. He was struggling with his control of the planet and of himself. She needed to guide him carefully before she or he got hurt.

"It was our people who discovered the thing and it was our people who dated it to before our race existed on the planet. Not the Federation."

"A trick," he said, sounding firm despite the preposterousness of the statement. "Cleverly planted to force us to be more closely linked to them. No doubt that insane old woman Rugan was part of the conspiracy."

Cuzar sighed and settled back. She had pushed him far enough. She then began asking about the relief and repair efforts, focusing him on concrete, productive issues. He began to calm down and she sighed in relief, but knew the situation was far from settled.

CHAPTER
8

Carol Abramowitz completed a second set of scans of the exposed pipework and its frayed, splintered wires. With the touch of a control, the tricorder's databanks were shared with the *da Vinci*'s computers.

Touching her restored combadge, she called to the starship. "Abramowitz to Soloman."

"Go ahead, Carol," the Bynar said.

"We don't have a lot of time so I'd like you to run the alien writing through the cultural databanks, looking for musical matches. We suspect it's more of a tonal than written language."

"Understood, stand by." He cut the signal and Carol let out a sigh. She had done what she could for the moment. The Evorans were an intriguing people and she wished there was sufficient time for her to do a proper job. Everything had been determined based on the most surface of impressions. She'd need a few weeks, totally without incident, to get a real feel

for the people. So far, her training and instincts had helped her, but she had come to a dead end. Without more facts or time or both, there was little left for her to do.

Times like this she wished she were one of those geniuses who could master many disciplines. From here on, it would fall to Sonya to salvage the situation. Understanding the language was nice, but right now, they needed a working power node to interface with the rest of the alien technology that had been keeping the planet from shaking apart. She'd been through something similar on Keorga only a few weeks ago. She, Bart, and Soloman had managed to pull a proverbial rabbit out of their hats then—she could only hope that history repeated itself.

She glanced over to see Sonya testing some of the exposed wiring to better understand the harmonics' frequency and power emissions. The commander seemed totally enthralled by the work, but the perspiration running down her cheeks showed just how tense the situation was becoming.

Bart, to his credit, was continuing to look at the rest of the exposed pipe, touching the raised letters—or notes?—and continuing his research. He seemed possessed, ignoring his personal fears and concentrating on the job, just as Sonya had advised. But then, once Bart started sinking his teeth into a linguistic conundrum, he could focus with the best of them.

Hawkins was studiously watching the now-recovered Onlith. As for Core Breach herself,

Corsi was taking a perimeter walk of the encampment to make sure there would be no other surprises.

It had become a waiting game and she was not good at waiting under circumstances like these.

Within ten minutes, though, she was signaled by the ship. Soloman began, without preamble, *"There's an amazing mathematical progression in the structure, so it took me longer to decipher than I thought."*

Carol laughed but encouraged Soloman to continue. Only a Bynar would think ten minutes was too long to decipher an unknown alien language.

"You were wrong, though," he continued.

"What do you mean?"

"It's not musical notes in lieu of a written language. This is a blend, one I would think is most elegant. There's not quite enough of a sample to fully understand it all but it matches no known Evoran language nor any in our own databanks."

"Anything in it that can help the commander?"

"Maybe. I'm transmitting the best approximation of the translation and she can decide for herself."

"Thanks, Soloman. Abramowitz out."

Within seconds her tricorder beeped, signaling that the transmission was complete, and she walked it over to Sonya, who was feeding instructions into the replicator.

"Read it to me, I've got to keep on this," she said with a small plea in her voice.

Carol dutifully read the translation, which dealt with amps and frequencies; all the while Gomez was bobbing her head up and down. It was almost comical to Abramowitz to watch her bob in rhythm with her reading.

As Sonya worked, Rugan had been inching closer to the group, her curiosity clearly getting the best of her. At one point Hawkins raised his phaser toward her, but Carol shook her head at him, and he lowered it.

"Damnedest thing I've ever seen," the scientist said.

"Well, it's new to us, too," Carol said.

"You see an alien artifact for the first time and in hours manage to decipher the language and even figure out how to repair it. I didn't even know what I was looking at."

"It's just the difference in technology," Carol said in a warm tone. She liked the scientist and didn't want to overplay the Federation's role. "Had you the same equipment . . ."

"No, I don't think so," Rugan said dejectedly. "I haven't a team like yours. I work with people scared of their own shadow. Most would rather keep their heads in the ground like the *sellow* birds."

"There must be more like you."

"Only if we can get the teachers to adopt new ways. So many young minds remain closed, so much waste . . ."

"When this is over, and your people discover the truth, that may be the spark they need. Don't give up on your own people."

"I try not to, but they disappoint me so often," Rugan said, moving over to get a closer view of Sonya's activity.

"Of course," Gomez exclaimed at that moment, startling the scientist. She quickly reprogrammed some numbers into the replicator and then activated it. Within seconds, a housing similar to the destroyed node appeared. If anything it was less appealing to look at than the original. Then she called up to the ship and asked Pattie to help supply her with various pieces of equipment.

"Want to explain what's going on?" Bart asked after a burst of activity.

"What?" Sonya looked up, almost as if she had forgotten her crewmates. She shook her head a moment. "These nodes seem to be the regulators. As the tectonic plates try to shift, the nodes draw power from the network and use the vibrations to either smooth the plate edges or disperse the vibrations from the actual shifts."

Sonya stopped to collect the equipment that had materialized by her side. Carol, fascinated, went over and began handing her the items, to move things along. "The node was destroyed, so there was nothing drawing power to stop the plates. Without the stress relief, the plates were free to move and took advantage. I need to confirm this, but my guess is Evora is one of the most unstable planets to sustain life that we've ever come across."

"And the only way to sustain that life was the network," Carol ventured.

"Right." Sonya sighed. "How do we explain to Helanoman that his entire race owes its very existence to some other, more benevolent race?"

Carol shook her head. "You don't. I don't think

you can get through to him. Someone needs to take this directly to the people."

"Let's get the situation under control first," Gomez said, and returned to her work. "I need to build and calibrate this before the aftershocks throw more of this network out of whack. We've only got about twenty minutes."

"I'm going down there," Gold said aloud as he stood up.

"Is that wise, sir?" Duffy asked.

"Wise? Probably not. But I'm not going to solve this by sitting on my *tuchis*. I need to be in the same room with that lunatic. You have the conn, Duffy. Whatever Gomez needs, she gets."

"Of course," Duffy said in a rush. "Shouldn't I try and talk you out of this?"

Gold paused and smiled. "You're welcome to try."

Duffy smiled back. "The captain shouldn't put himself in danger. Besides, the last time you left me in charge, I almost started a war with the Tholians."

"But you didn't, and that counts for a lot, Duffy. Objection overruled. Take the conn."

"Yes, sir," Duffy said, moving the command chair without hesitation.

Within moments, Gold was emerging from the turbolift near the transporter room. He stopped long enough to grab a phaser and then stood on the platform. His lessons at Starfleet Academy and his experience over the years showed that yes, in many—hell, *most*—cases, it made sense to keep the captain out of harm's way. But he also knew that there came a time the captain had to insert himself into the thick of it—and this definitely qualified.

"Any interference from the network near the capitol?"

Feliciano checked a readout and shook his head. "No, sir, we're all clear."

"Very well, beam me down right outside the regent's office. Energize."

Moments later, the captain was standing before the small, polished wood door. Three very startled Evorans were looking up at him. "We can do this the easy way or hard way," Gold said to them. "I either stun you into submission or you let me stroll into the office."

The Evorans stared at Gold's holstered phaser and then his imposing figure. Then back at the phaser. Within seconds they began to back down the corridor, refusing to turn their backs to Gold but also not challenging him.

To keep Helanoman guessing, Gold merely reached for the handle and pushed the door open.

Sure enough, Helanoman was communicating in agitated tones to some subordinate and barely reacted to the door's sound. Cuzar, though, looked up immediately and her face ran through a variety of reactions that amused the captain. Finally, she settled on a look imploring him for help and he nodded, giving her a reassuring smile.

"I thought I'd bring you the truth myself," he said in a calm tone.

The Onlith leader whirled about in surprise. He

reached for his own weapon, but Gold had already crossed the room without fear. At no point had he reached for his own weapon, and he certainly did not want to invite trouble. Standing barely two feet from the Evoran, Gold looked down and shook his head warningly.

"Understand me: if I wanted to, I could have brought a security detachment with me and you would be in custody. But I do not wish to interfere with a planet's sovereignty any more than I have to. You and Cuzar can wrestle for the title of regent when this is over—or better yet, put it to a vote, since you seem so sure that the people are on your side. But right now, you must listen to reason."

Helanoman was seething but Gold spotted the fear in his eyes.

"That node you destroyed allowed the quakes to begin. I have people there now trying to stop more from arriving. Your blind arrogance has put the people you hope to lead in danger."

"You put that device there to make us beholden to you!"

"If you believe that, fine. When this is done, if you remain in power and want us gone, we'll warp out of orbit. Right now, though, you're a Federation protectorate and I am here in response to your people's call for help. Want it or not, you will be receiving that help."

Gold walked over to an empty chair and dragged it to Cuzar's desk. He went and got a second one, exposing his back to Helanoman, letting the man know that there was a certain amount of trust being placed in him—though he supposed Helanoman might interpret the gesture as an insult. The captain settled in the second chair and gestured to Helanoman to take the other one.

"While my people work, shall we discuss resolving this power struggle?"

CHAPTER
9

"**D**ammit, the flux capacitor won't fit!"

Gomez wiped at her damp forehead with her sleeve and bit her lower lip as she tried to figure out how to cram all the needed technical equipment into the node. Had they managed to crack it open earlier, she'd have been able to check the level of miniaturization required. Right now, she was still guessing at what was needed to modulate the tremors. In her mind, an imaginary clock was continuing to tick down until the first estimated aftershock. If Pattie was right, it was going to be a rough ride, enough to possibly ruin her work.

Under other circumstances, she'd have asked for additional help—Pattie, Kieran, an entire team—but the node was so *small* that more than one person working on it was impractical.

She slowed her breathing and forced her racing mind to focus on the single task in front of her. The capacitor needed to handle input and output feeds, both of which might be trimmable. Reaching into her equipment case, she pulled out crimpers that neatly cut the input feed. Sonya again tried to fit the capacitor into the new node, but it still didn't fit. This time, rather than curse, she trimmed the output feed and refitted the device.

"Much better," she said to herself. It didn't matter to her if she spoke out loud or not; what mattered was that she maintain her cool. Focus was required and that meant ignoring whatever else was happening. She had to trust Corsi and Hawkins to maintain order, allowing her to do the work required. Her life might have been on the line but after months on the *da Vinci*, she would not have it any other way. The S.C.E. afforded her more challenges than the work on any starship, even more than on the fabled *Enterprise*. And working on the *da Vinci* gave her a chance to also be in a command position. Her career had certainly taken some interesting twists but there was nothing to complain about. Personally, she had even managed to rekindle her relationship with Kieran. What did she have to complain about?

By way of answer, Evora chose that moment to move rather violently.

Gomez tumbled to her knees, and her arms went reflexively over her head. She cursed herself, realizing she needed to protect the node first. A moment later she felt Rugan tumble into her; the scientist had been leaning in close, watching the repair work and staying silent. Gomez held on to the old woman for a moment, making sure she was safe. As aftershocks went, this was pretty mild, lasting a handful of seconds and nowhere near as severe as expected.

"You okay down there?" It was Abramowitz, who seemed fine herself.

"Peachy," she answered, looking over to the Evoran scientist, who nodded just once. Gomez turned her attention back to the node. With the capacitor now in place, she could concentrate on the phase modulator. But first, she was still a commander with a team. "How's everything topside?"

"Peachy," Carol replied with a grin. "Everything's under control so just worry about the network."

Another aftershock rolled across the land and this time Abramowitz fell forward, tumbling into the pit and landing hard beside the node. Rugan herself was thrown into the makeshift device, cracking a connection to the pipe network. Gomez had tucked herself into a ball, letting bits of rock and silt cover her back and shoulders.

This one lasted longer than the first one, and seemed more violent. Gomez gritted her teeth and stood over Abramowitz's prone-but-conscious body. She'd be black and blue for days after all this.

"I'm fine," she said as she spit out dirt.

Rugan indicated she too was fine and was extremely apologetic for breaking Gomez's work. The engineer looked at the cracked connection, shook her head, and swiftly reached into her kit and grabbed a hydrospanner. There had better be a breather before the next shock if she expected to complete her work and even have time to test the unit.

Five minutes later, she had everything reassembled and it all fit together. It was ugly as sin, twice as bulky as the original node, but ready to work. There was just the one tiny matter of determining the right frequency.

"Bart," she called. In moments, Faulwell's cheerful face hung over the lip of the excavation.

"Did that translation from Soloman contain the original frequency?"

Faulwell blinked and then consulted his tricorder. He frowned and thumbed the readout up and down, and Gomez began to fret. She needed to set it at something and she'd much rather not guess.

"Nothing here," he finally said. He frowned. "It might be built into the language itself. If it's at least partly musical in nature, then it's set at a certain pitch."

Gomez shrugged; it made some sense. She looked at Soloman's translation and then compared it with the vibrations Pattie had managed to record from orbit. Sure enough, they were close enough for her to make a very educated guess. She began inputting the instructions.

"What makes you so certain this will work?" Rugan asked.

"Well, I've had plenty of experience with repair work, and my instincts tell me we're on the right course. Am I absolutely certain it will work? Of course not. It's alien technology and that brings lots of unknowns with it. But right now, I've got to go with my instincts. Here goes nothing," she said. With that, she pressed two studs protruding from the new node housing. Ruby lights blinked on and everyone could hear an audible whine build before surpassing human hearing.

Gomez tapped her combadge and called the *da Vinci*. "Pattie, what do the sensors read?"

"Just a moment, Commander," the Nasat replied. The moment stretched to several and Gomez paced her small trench, eager to get up top and away from the dig entirely.

Abramowitz and Rugan were standing side by side, silent. Gomez looked up to see Faulwell and Corsi peering down from above.

"The frequencies match," P8 Blue announced. *"The patch is working and the network is no longer straining."*

"Is it enough to stop the aftershocks?"

"Probably mute them but stop them, no," P8 said.

"We'll stay here to see that the equipment holds during the next shock," Gomez said. "Out." With that, she reached up and was happily pulled to the surface by her colleagues.

"My ship informs me a replacement device has worked successfully," Gold told Cuzar and Helanoman.

They had been sitting around the desk, with the Onlith leader blustering on about all of the Federation's many mistakes. Gold had to suffer this in silence, letting the Evoran man have his say so that when Gold finally spoke, Helanoman might actually listen.

"Are you certain this will stop more earthquakes?"

"Regent, until something occurs, everything is merely speculation."

"We did record one aftershock already," Cuzar pointed out, clearly hoping she was wrong. Gold admired the woman and liked her quiet style.

"Of course, that was before activation. We just have to wait and see."

"I hate waiting."

"Part of being a good leader, Helanoman, is being able to wait without losing one's mind," Gold answered. The smaller man had nothing to say in response. He seemed to ignore the comments and just sat. Cuzar shrugged her shoulders in a universal signal of resignation.

"Gomez to Gold."

"Go ahead, Commander. Is everything fine at the dig?"

"Waiting on the next shock wave, but I'm optimistic. I wanted to come make my report in person."

"Good thought. If Helanoman does not mind . . ." The captain looked over to the Onlith leader, who just stared.

"I don't think I want to wait that long."

"Oh, that's not a problem. Go ahead, Commander."

Moments later, Gomez materialized in the regent's office, which was beginning to feel crowded. She was covered with dust, dirt, and something that he suspected was a lubricant. Her hair was a mess but there was no denying the triumphant look in her eyes. Helanoman just stared at her, more with surprise than anger. No doubt this further proved his point that contamination was continuing.

"Report."

"While we've translated some of the language, we have no idea who built the network," Gomez said. "Abramowitz's best explanation is that they were a benevolent race, similar to the Preservers, and they . . ."

"Preservers?" Cuzar asked.

Gold explained. "An ancient race, long gone; but they built protective devices on many worlds we have discovered. We know very little about them, actually." Helanoman seemed pleased by the lack of knowledge.

"Sensor readings from the ship seem to indicate Evora is a very unstable planet," Gomez continued, pausing then to check for reactions. The captain appreciated the gesture of respect. Neither Evoran seemed to know how to handle the information. He nodded for her to continue.

"The geological readings Rugan took at the dig help confirm the hypothesis. This planet has undergone major geologic upheaval since it was formed. That's why entire species were wiped out in a seeming blink of the eye."

"And this mystery race . . . they built the stabilizers?"

"Yes, Regent," Gomez said softly. "Some millennia back, after the last quake wiped out the animal life, they undertook the task. Stabilizing the planet allowed life finally to flourish and endure. Until now, your people barely experienced a tremor, thanks to their ingenuity."

"How does the system work?" Gold asked.

"That, I'm less sure about," his engineer answered. "Clearly, we believe the planet's core is providing the power source. How the device knows to emit the right harmonics is beyond me." What went unsaid was her desire to find out how, but Gold knew that would be impossible without compromising the ancient system.

Cuzar sat, staring blankly at the screen in front of her. Helanoman also seemed to be staring into space, and for a moment Gold actually felt some sympathy for him. His entire belief system had been challenged and found wanting. He would now have to live with the notion that the Evoran people did owe their very existence to another race.

"Whatever race chose to do this did so without asking for a price. They did it because it was the right thing to do. It could be the biggest good deed I have ever witnessed," Gold said. "This doesn't change anything. All of your accomplishments, like developing warp drive, are entirely your own doing. The aliens' work ended millennia ago, so there's nothing to be ashamed about, Helanoman. Yes, it'll take time to adjust, and the Federation can send teachers or historians to help with the adjust-ment—or not, if that's what you prefer. Nothing will be easy, but life wouldn't be interesting if it was."

"I knew we were right to seek an alliance within the galactic community," Cuzar said. "When we took that first warp flight two years ago, I hoped we would find friends, not enemies. What shall we do now, Helanoman?"

The man continued to sit, his eyes staring and his expression unreadable. The regent gave him time to gather his thoughts and wits. Gold and Gomez looked on sympathetically, but remained where they were. This was not their affair, the captain recognized, so it required patience.

"Helanoman?"

Finally, the more massive Evoran blinked and shrugged his shoulders, a statue coming to life. He turned his head to the regent and simply said, "You win."

"This isn't about winning or losing," Cuzar said, showing her grace. "Our people made a collective decision to join the Federation family and your followers seek to undermine that. Now that we know the truth, what do you intend to do?"

"I will . . . I will ask my people to stand down and let the planet function as it has," he said. "I will then submit myself to you for punishment."

Cuzar let that hang in the air for a few moments, and Gold was curious to see how she would handle this. She didn't seem to be milking the moment for pleasure. He was pleased by that.

"There needs be some punishment, yes. We can't have people leading coups without any consequences. Still, you acted based on your beliefs, not because you sought power in and of itself. We shall let the judiciary review and make a decision. Please, give the word to the Onlith, tell them it's over."

"Yes," he said sadly. "It's over." He turned away and began speaking into his communications device.

Cuzar finally rose from her chair and approached

the captain. She moved gracefully and with purpose. "I cannot thank you enough, Captain. You and your crew saved my world."

"We fix things," Gold said, smiling. "Usually, it's just equipment but it seems we may have helped repair this rift among you. If you'd like, I can stay and help with the restoration of your control."

"No thank you, Captain," Cuzar said proudly. "We have made do on our own long enough that this will not require any additional help. While I welcome our place in your family, I remain committed to the Evorans finding our own way. The Onlith and the rest of the government have other issues that need resolving before we can consider this finished. You did more than enough just getting these discussions started."

"Good," said Gold. "I'll have my crew return to the ship and we'll prepare to leave orbit."

"Will Rugan be allowed to continue her work at the site?" Gomez asked.

"Oh yes," Cuzar said. "There's too much to learn about our world. In fact, Captain, we may invite experts from the Federation to observe or help . . . later. Maybe we can repay your kindness with a discovery about this race that helped us."

Gold smiled at the notion and considered the matter well on its way to being resolved.

"*Yew-cheen chef-faw,*" Cuzar said.

"*Yew-cheen chef-faw,*" Gold replied, pleased he got the pronunciation right at last.

CHAPTER
10

"I hate mysteries," Corsi said as the away team returned to the *da Vinci*.

"Yeah, just as we solve one thing, there's a new wrinkle," Faulwell added. "Doesn't seem right."

"The universe is a big place, we'll never understand it all and the sooner you accept that, the better you will sleep at night."

"Thank you, Carol."

"Don't mention it."

As they stepped off the platform, Gomez entered the room and greeted her team with a smile. "Well, how badly did we bang you up this time, Vance?"

"Not too badly at all," he said with a grin. "Won't even need to see Emmett this time. Which is kind of a shame, really, since we were just getting to know one another."

"You can tell this guy's been banged around too much if he's starting to build a relationship with the EMH," Faulwell quipped.

"Captain wants your logs and reports by 1000 tomorrow. Right now he suggests you get cleaned up and have some rest," Gomez said, slipping into command mode.

As they group started to leave the room and spill into the corridor, Gomez sidled up to Corsi and said in a low tone, "I dislike unresolved issues, too, but it's just something we have to live with."

"Just not something I have to like."

"Of course not," Gomez said. The group headed toward the door, but she stopped them by saying, "You all did good work down there. I'm proud of you all. Now, go freshen up and meet me in the mess. I want to tell you all about this report I just read about how they stopped the uprising on Rigel II."

"Now, that's more like it," the security officer said. "A problem *and* a solution."

OATHS

Glenn Hauman

Acknowledgments

First and foremost, my medical advisor, Dr. Matthew Sims, who went above and beyond the call in answering my questions. Any errors that crept in are my fault, not his.

Keith DeCandido, who through strange circumstances is responsible for most of my professional writing sales to date.

David Mack, who spent a lot of time working with me on the last Plague I was exposed to. I'm still not sure if he's forgiven me for introducing him to John Ordover.

And finally, my own twin towers, Lisa Sullivan and Brandy Hauman.

"It is not the oath that makes us believe the man, but the man the oath."

—Aeschylus

"Healing is a matter of time, but it is sometimes also a matter of opportunity."

——Hippocrates

CHAPTER
1

Lense focused.

The sickbay of the *da Vinci* was quiet, with Vance Hawkins the only patient in, being treated for a fractured ulna and torn ligament injury sustained during a security drill. Dr. Elizabeth Lense was ignoring him. She continued to sit in her office and stare at the computer screen on her desk.

Emmett, the Emergency Medical Hologram treating the injury, closed the tricorder. "You are free to go, Mr. Hawkins. Your injury will be fine by the end of the week. May I suggest that you be more careful next time?"

"Sorry. Occupational hazard."

"Yes, well, perhaps a change of occupation might be better for you. You've visited sickbay more than any other member of security. You may wish to consider a less hazardous line of work."

"What? And give up show business?"

"I'm sorry, I don't quite get the reference."

"Never mind. Doctor, is there anything else I should do?"

"No," Emmett said. "Avoid overuse of the arm, and general rest should be fine."

"Doctor?" He looked past Emmett and addressed Dr. Lense.

"Hmm?" Dr. Lense looked up, distracted.

"Is there anything else I should be doing for my arm?"

"No, what Emmett said is just fine."

"Okay. Thanks. And thank you, Emmett."

"You're more than welcome. Always happy to see you. Not happy to see you hurt, of course, but—"

"I know what you meant, you big lug. Don't use too much electricity."

Emmett watched him leave, then said, "Dr. Lense, I've filed a full report. Is there anything else you need me for?"

"No, Emmett. Switch off, but reactivate if anybody else comes in. Is that clear?"

"Yes, Doctor." Emmett vanished.

"Good boy," she said to the empty air.

She went back to her terminal, tapping occasionally at different places on the screen. Eleven minutes later, her communicator beeped. *"Gold to Lense."*

"Go ahead, Captain."

"Doctor, I'd like to see you in my ready room."

"Certainly. I can be up by the end of the—"

"Now, Doctor, if you don't mind."

Lense hesitated. "All right. I'll be there in five minutes."

"Thank you. Gold out."

Resigned, Dr. Lense got up to leave—abandoning the problem she had been working on and was so close to solving.

She didn't see that by moving the red nine to the black ten, she would free up the ace of clubs.

Captain's Personal Log, Stardate 53661.9.

I've just summoned Dr. Lense to my office. Actually, "ordered" is probably the correct word.

I hate to actually pull rank on my crew. The fact that I have just done so merely indicates to me that my course of action is an appropriate one.

Because of the nature of that action, I am going to record the transcript of our upcoming conversation here. Should it be necessary later, I will transfer it to an official log entry, although it's my hope that can be avoided.

Times like this, I wish Rachel was here. She always reads people better than I do. It was good to see her, Daniel, Esther, and the twins—not to mention Esther's new beau, Khor, son of Lantar. *That* meeting went off without a—

The doorchime just rang. Starting transcript now.

TRANSCRIPT STARTS

G: Come.

L: Sir.

G: Come in, Doctor. Have a seat.

L: Thank you.

G: A drink?

L: Nothing for me, thanks.

G: Congratulations, Doctor. You're the first officer on board the *da Vinci* I've actually had to call in for a performance review.

L: Really, sir.

G: Yes. And would you like to know why? [Pause.] It's because I know almost nothing new about you—nothing that isn't already in your official file.

L: I see.

G: I never see you outside of meetings that I call. I don't see you in the mess hall. I don't see you interacting with the crew, except in a professional capacity—and lately, I've been getting reports you haven't even been doing that. I understand that you've been letting the Emergency Medical Hologram do most of your patient work.

L: Yes, I have. Emmett's supposed to learn procedure, and there's no other way to do that than to let him do the work, interacting with patients and situations in the field.

G: The specifications on this EMH gave him a huge medical database. Yes, it had the personality of a first-year resident, but that was to make it seem eager and helpful. Not burned out and abrasive.

L: Well, that may be what was planned. He's still rough around the edges. I believe he needed real-world experience, and I've been giving it to him. And to be fair, you don't have the expertise in the field to make that decision as to his medical skills and expertise.

G: We're digressing, Doctor. This isn't about the EMH. It's about you. I'm beginning to think that *you're* the one that's burned out.

L: I see.

G: You know, I have records here going all the way back to your time in the Academy. I have this glowing recommendation from the head of Starfleet Medical at the time, Dr. Crusher. Have you ever seen it?

L: No. I only took one class with her, then she went back to duty on the *Enterprise*.

G: Let me quote: "Elizabeth Lense is one of the fastest studies I've ever come across. Brilliant and incisive diagnosis. . . ." An outstanding school career, first in your class at the Academy, all of it leading to being appointed CMO of the *U.S.S. Lexington* right out of Starfleet Medical. Unprecedented in Starfleet history in peacetime. A truly great honor . . . and then you end up here.

L: Here? Captain Gold, the *da Vinci* is a fine ship—

G: A damn fine ship, and thank you for the compliment. But after serving on the *Lexington*, with a crew complement of hundreds, this is a bit of a reduction of duties, wouldn't you say? Going down to a ship with only forty crewmembers? A ship so small you go from a suite of your own to sharing a room? A ship so small . . . that it doesn't even have a ship's counselor.

L: Pardon me, but could I take you up on that offer for a glass of water?

G: Certainly. You don't mind if I continue?

L: Could I stop you?

G: Not particularly.

L: Well. Go ahead, then.

G: Thank you. Computer, a glass of water, please. [Replicator hum.] Here you go.

L: Thank you, sir.

G: Now then, back to the matter at hand. Over the past few weeks, you've been less and less engaged with this crew and with your duties. I noted that you've been spending more time eating in sickbay than your quarters or the mess hall. You're in a bad way, Doctor, and it's beginning to seriously affect your work.

L: That's absurd.

G: You don't believe me? Gold to Emergency Medical Hologram.

EMH: Sickbay, Emmett here. May I help you, Captain?

G: Emmett, I need a diagnosis. Would you say that Dr. Lense has been behaving erratically lately? A little off-kilter?

L: Emmett—

G: Pipe down, Doctor. Or else.

E: Captain, is Dr. Lense with you? Does she require medical assistance?

G: No, nothing at the moment. I was merely asking if she'd seemed off-kilter to you.

E: Dr. Lense has seemed . . . fatigued, lately. Somewhat listless. She has shown markedly diminished interest in almost all activities most of the day. I would suspect a degree of sleep disorder based on observation.

G: Your diagnosis?

E: Her symptoms are characteristic of a depressive episode. I couldn't attest to state of mind or causes without further examination.

G: Thank you.

E: Is there any other way I can be of assistance, Captain?

G: Not at this time. Gold out.

L: [Unintelligible] observant, I'll give him that.

G: Well, Doctor? Do you disagree with your colleague's conclusion?

L: He's not a colleague, he's a database with delusions of grandeur. A mechanic of flesh instead of clockworks.

G: So, wrong that makes him? Doctor, you

know he's right. You finagled your way onto a ship that didn't have a counselor. I can't prove it, but you know it and I know it. I can only assume that's because you don't want to deal with your problems, and I can respect that up until the point where they become my problems. And a nonfunctional CMO is my problem.

L: So what are you going to do about it?

G: Well, that's another problem. Standard operating procedure would probably be to have you taken off active duty and sent for a psych workup. But that would require us getting you to a counselor who could do that, and probably would entail leaving you at the nearest starbase for a month. Either our scheduled maintenance visit to Sherman's Planet would have to be delayed or I'd have to give you a shuttlecraft, and we only have the two. Either way, I'd be without a chief medical officer for who knows how long, and you'd almost certainly be reassigned, with a nasty mark on your service record. Your career might never recover. I don't want to do that and neither, I suppose, do you. So we're going to try and avoid the whole magilla.

L: Sir?

G: Instead, we're going to have our own little counseling sessions right here.

You and me, at least once a week for the foreseeable future, in this office, with all conversations kept out of the official record as long as things go well. And we're going to talk and try to get to the bottom of this.

L: You're no doctor, and you're not a counselor either.

G: No, I'm not. But I'm your commanding officer. And I'm the one you have to convince that you're not just going through the motions, that you really are in shape to serve on board my ship.

L: Fine. Whatever.

G: You're resenting this.

L: I don't have to talk to you.

G: Actually, yes, you do. Complain all you want, this is what we're going to do.

L: I could invoke my Seventh Guarantee rights.

G: You do that and I'll make all this official, and have you transferred off this ship, downchecked for active duty, and sent for an immediate psych exam. Playing this by the book is not the way you want to go, believe me.

L: You realize that I could have you removed from command for medical reasons.

G: You'd have to show cause eventually, Doctor, or face charges of mutiny. And before that, you'd still have to deal with Gomez—I guess you'd have to throw

Gomez into the brig too. And then
Duffy. And so on. But you know, it
doesn't even matter. You'd never even
go as far as relieving me of command. I
know it and you know it. But I don't
think you know why, do you? [Pause.]
It's because you don't want to take the
responsibility for making the decision.

L: Maybe I'll just be happy getting rid of
you.

G: Our first session will be tomorrow at
0800. Dismissed.

L: I—

G: You're dismissed, Doctor.

TRANSCRIPT ENDS

Well . . . that was fun. I can just imagine how
our sessions are going to go.

CHAPTER
2

Sherman's Planet (so named, according to conflicting stories in the Memory Alpha databanks, either to repay a staggeringly large bar tab, to serve as a warning that a particularly obnoxious individual lived there, or to impress a woman) was in an area of space first mapped by Terrans in 2067 by John Burke, the chief astronomer of the Royal Academy of England. There had been a battle in orbit around nearby Donatu V in 2242 between the Federation and the Klingons over settlements in the sector, with inconclusive results which didn't really become clarified until the Organians came along and imposed a sort of unilateral peace between the two sides twenty years later. It was colonized by the Federation under the dictates of the Organian Peace Treaty. There had been a bit of unpleasantness with the Klingon Empire involving espionage, a famine, and a poisoned grain shipment, but it was a minor footnote to the early frontier days of the planet.

The Klingons never got around to that neck of the galaxy after the incident, as they appeared to have developed an aversion to the area—almost as if they were allergic to something.

The planet itself was quite hostile to most Earth plants, with only a few exceptions—fortunately for them, one of the exceptions was the grape. Within a few years of settling, superlative vintages were coming off the planet. Some of the native flora blended well with the Terran grapes, creating unheard-of varieties of wine. All in all, the colonists were able to eke out a comfortable existence—certainly until replicator technology had advanced enough so that a comfortable existence was almost a given for any citizen of the Federation who wanted it.

The human population of the planet had grown rather quickly in the century since, with an estimated three million people living there. Of course, on a planet about the size of Venus, that left a lot of room for people to spread out. It was rare for a family to have less than a few dozen acres of land under their domain—even if that land was still mostly rocks and trees.

With a planetary infrastructure built up after the major power problems of recrystallizing dilithium had been solved, people enjoyed the capacity to spread out. Personal shuttlecraft and the like made it easy to travel to the next town, even if that town was three hundred miles away. And with almost every family having their own on-site replicators, there was no real danger of going without anything. There would be no worry of a repeat of the famine that endangered the colony, though the famine did make for some entertaining stories told by grandparents to their young ones—at least, entertaining to the grandparents.

All in all, war and famine seemed like things of the past. Life was safe and comfortable. Nobody wanted for much, nobody needed too much. The biggest problem the planet's administrators had was that more and more young people wanted to "transport off this boring rock" and see the galaxy—a problem endemic throughout most of the Federation's worlds nowadays.

Abe Auerbach had a similar problem—he wanted off this rock too, and he'd just gotten there.

For the fifth time that day, he cursed his mother for deciding to resettle on Sherman's Planet. Now he was stuck with coming out here from a civilized part of the galaxy to help her with what she called "his inheritance." He called it a great big bunch of hilly land in the boondocks. His taste ran more to beaches—preferably on Risa, with a nice cool drink in hand. But she had decided to move back to Armstrong City, and she had insisted her dutiful son should be the one to settle her affairs on Sherman's Planet, which included closing up and selling the house she'd lived in.

Once he'd gotten out there, Abe discovered his mom had let the place go to seed in her old age, and it was in such a condition that nobody would take it off his hands without some major renovations. Which was what he'd been doing for the last two months.

He'd done most of the home repair that he could in the winter, but now that spring was here, he was finally ready to put in that swimming pool. He'd rented an industrial phaser for the job and had already cleared the trees and brush, and now he was using it to disintegrate a hole in the earth. He'd decided on a deep pool, and had excavated about four and a half meters down. Unfortunately, before he could finish, it started to rain, and so he put it aside for another day. He figured it would be good for the rain to tamp down the newly exposed soil, anyway.

The rain and the dirt brought to light (literally) something that hadn't been seen on the surface of Sherman's Planet for about three thousand years.

Abe never knew about it. He was going to start lining the pool when the rain stopped, but by then he'd gotten a cold and hadn't really felt up to doing it. He just holed himself up in the house and watched old comedy vids, but switched to dramas after the laughing started provoking severe coughing fits.

Captain's Personal Log, Stardate 53663.3.

The *da Vinci* is oddly quiet. Most of the crew is off the ship, either engaged in various fixer-up projects on Sherman's Planet or engaging in some much-needed shore leave. Left on the ship, there's only myself, who just had shore leave a week ago; Wong at conn keeping us from falling out of orbit; Stevens, who begged off leave because "somebody had to run the ship here"; Hawkins, because Corsi insisted on leaving somebody on board, and Hawkins used up his leave time after the incident on the *Debenture of Triple-Lined Latinum* in any event.

And Dr. Lense.

I was actually of two minds as to keeping Lense up here. On the one hand, shore leave might be good for her. On the other hand, wandering around in a funk during a leave might draw even more attention to her, which I'm studiously trying to avoid. Besides, with the ship pretty much empty, it allows me to conduct a lengthier session with her, without drawing grief from the crew.

I'm keeping a copy of our sessions here in my personal log, to help collect my own thoughts and observations and to have a record I can hand to Starfleet Medical, if necessary. I'm hoping it won't come to that—but after today's session, I think I begin to realize just how damaged she might be. These quotes should illustrate.

TRANSCRIPT STARTS

L: Hello, Captain.

G: Hello, Doctor. Good to see you.

L: If you say so.

G: Have a seat. Water?

L: Yes. You've almost gotten this down to a routine, haven't you?

G: I hope so. My grandmother told me good manners should always be routine.

L: How sweet. What was her opinion on prying into someone's personal life?

G: She wholeheartedly practiced it.

L: Of course she did.

G: I *nudzh*. It's what I do. If you prefer, I'm invoking captain's privilege. You don't like it, find another counselor. Shall we get started?

L: Sure, why not.

G: So.

L: So.

G: Where would you like to start?

L: I wouldn't.

G: No, no, no. Not an option.

L: Of course not. Pick a point, then. I have no idea.

G: All right. Why do you call the EMH "Emmett"?

L: [Laughs.] You don't know? I thought it was obvious.

G: I'm slow to understand sometimes. Why don't you enlighten me?

L: He's an Emergency Medical Technician. An EMT. You know, E-M-T. "Emmett." Get it?

G: Oh, of course. I should have realized. Okay, new topic. When did you first decide you wanted to be a doctor?

L: I don't know . . . I was maybe thirteen or so. The competition for ballerinas was too intense.

G: Surely competition didn't bother you?

L: No, it didn't. I was kidding. Okay . . . it was something I was good at. I picked it up like that. It was easy to envision how a body was all put together, and how making a few changes here and there could affect so many things, make so many things happen.

G: And from all accounts, you were excellent at it.

L: Yes, a true idiot savant.

G: Oh, now come on. Aren't you being needlessly hard on yourself?

L: Maybe. But I am a good doctor. I'm supposed to be able to make these brilliant diagnoses.

G: And yet, we agree your performance has been off its peak recently. When do you think it started?

L: A little surprise happened about three years ago, when I was on the *Lexington*. It turned out that the salutatorian of my class, Julian Bashir, was genetically enhanced.

G: I've heard of him. He's still the chief medical officer of Deep Space 9, correct?

L: Yes. I understand his father pled guilty to the illegal genetic engineering charges and was sent to prison. Since it happened to Julian as a child and he was shown to be perfectly capable of functioning in normal society, he was allowed to keep his license and commission.

G: That was my understanding as well. So what does all this have to do with you? Was he a friend?

L: Julian? I didn't even know he existed in med school. Until we met on DS9 a few years after we got out, I thought he was someone else entirely—an Andorian, in fact. And considering what he's done since . . . well, he didn't do it, directly.

G: I'm not following.

L: Captain, I outperformed a genetically enhanced human. That's like beating a Gorn at arm wrestling. It's unheard of.

G: And yet you kept up with him. That's impressive work.

L: Yes. Starfleet thought so too. That's why I was investigated.

G: Investigated? There's none of this in your files.

L: There damn well better not be. I made sure that it was all taken out. It was a baseless accusation. But it still made a mess out of my life. Here we were, in the middle of the war, and we get a request to dock at Starbase 314. Captain Eberling called me into his ready room, and there were two security officers there from the starbase. He said, "These are Lieutenants Cioffi and Shvak. They need to bring you onto the starbase and ask some questions." And I was carried off to a lovely little suite inside the station where I had everything but a way to open the door. The starbase commander was a Phil Selden, and I stayed a month in the Selden Arms while they tried to prove that I was also genetically enhanced.

I wasn't even told about Julian for the first two weeks. I had no idea what they were digging for. My family history was investigated eight ways from Sunday; I found out later that my mother had been detained and investigated as well. They were convinced I was covering up. They talked about sending me away to the Institute where they keep all the other people who were genetically enhanced—they alternated that with threats of criminal proceedings. It took a month of combing over my back history before they would let me go back to active duty. And of course, the *Lexington* was long gone.

G: They left you behind.

L: They were ordered to the front lines.

G: They still left you behind.

L: It was orders. There was a war on. Surely, Captain, you understand.

G: Yes. But I can't imagine you liked it.

L: By the time I could catch up with the *Lexington*, two-thirds of the crew had been killed in battle or rotated off the ship, including Captain Eberling—he

died in one of the first skirmishes of the
war. So I never got a chance for an apology from him.

G: What did he owe you an apology for?

L: For not supporting one of his officers.
For jumping to conclusions.

G: I see. Sorry for interrupting.

L: I never got to say good-bye to any
of them. Gaines, Leff, Bowdren,
Twistekey—gone. When I came back, I
didn't know who half the crew was on
the ship. They didn't know me, either;
they thought I was some rookie freshly
promoted. Commander—sorry, *Captain*
Anderson was promoted to the center
chair from XO, and she and I never got
along well. She kept insisting I call her
"Heather."

G: Did you feel like you let them down?

L: What do you mean?

G: I mean, do you feel that if you were still
there on the ship, you would have been
able to keep those crewmembers alive?

L: I—Maybe. I don't know.

G: Your staff was, I assume, more than
competent; I doubt you would have
accepted less. You couldn't have done
more if you were there.

L: You don't know that. I don't know that.

G: Yes, you do, Elizabeth.

L: Do you know what the hell of it is? He
flubbed the question.

G: I'm sorry, what question?

L: A question during the oral section of the finals. If Bashir hadn't mistaken a pre-ganglionic fiber for a postganglionic nerve, he would've been valedictorian instead of me.

G: You didn't crack, and he—

L: You're missing the point. Preganglionic fibers and postganglionic nerves aren't anything alike. Any first-year medical student can tell them apart. He purposely gave the wrong answer. He flubbed it.

G: Oh.

L: Now do you see?

G: Why do you think he did it?

L: Well, I can't imagine it was the pressure of the exams. I think he was trying to hide that he was genetically enhanced. He was lying. And I was caught up in his lie. I'm sorry, I'd like to stop now. This isn't doing me any good. May I be dismissed, sir?

G: Yes. But I'd still like to hear about your experiences on the *Lexington* after you resumed your post there. May we try to continue this tomorrow?

L: Make it the day after tomorrow.

G: Two days then. Dismissed.

TRANSCRIPT ENDS

For what it's worth, I think I see a trend—there's a certain theme of guilt over unearned rewards. She feels she didn't deserve to be valedictorian, and she feels she didn't deserve to live when so many others on her ship didn't.

Of course, this doesn't give me any idea what to *do* about it.

I'm not sure how much more I can do here, other than just listen to her vent. She either has to make changes on her own, or with the help of people much more qualified than myself. And doing that may only make things worse.

CHAPTER
3

"Jubilee, you are a bad influence."

"Coming from you, Doctor, that is a compliment. Don't tell me you've never slipped a patient sweets before."

"Yes, but I keep it to one a patient. You spoil them. Just because 'Candy Striper' is a term for volunteers doesn't mean you have to go overboard."

"Well, the kids look so cute when they sniffle. I can't help myself."

"At this rate, we're going to run out of candy."

"Dr. Tyler, that's not because I'm handing out too much candy per child."

"I know. Have we gotten any of the lab results back?"

"They should be done by now. Let me finish my tea and I'll check."

"Never mind, Jube. I'll get it. How's your throat?"

"Getting sorer. I don't know what I caught from those kids, but it's a dilly."

"You could take an extra hour off and get a nap, you know."

"No, you're shorthanded enough as it is. This bug has already laid up half the medical staff, and you're getting more people checking in. This is a bad one, whatever it is."

"I hear you. Well, we do what we—"

"Attention. All available staff personnel please report to the operating amphitheater at once."

"Any ideas, Doctor?"

"Not a one."

Dr. Ambrose stood in the operating theater, looking up at the half-full gallery. He noted ruefully that the number of people in the room wasn't going to get any larger—*it's only going to get smaller from here,* he thought to himself.

He addressed the room. "Thank you all for coming. Ladies and gentlemen, we have a dire emergency on our hands."

A picture flashed on the screen. "This was Abraham Auerbach. He came to Sherman's about two months ago from Earth, according to Customs. He was brought into the hospital three days ago, complaining of severe chest pains, stomach cramping, coughing, and vomiting blood. He'd been suffering from what he thought was a very bad cold for the last three weeks. He died twenty-three hours ago of severe sepsis with multiorgan failure, primarily in the lungs. Our autopsy revealed many of the organs were necrotic." Dr. Ambrose flicked to images of the organs. A quiet rumble could be heard from the upper decks.

"There is no immediately apparent explanation for this. He had a clean bill of health when he came to the planet. There have been twenty-seven additional cases from all over the world admitted with similar symptoms two days ago. We have had an additional one hundred and fifty-seven cases admitted today. We—" and he started to cough a dry, hacking cough that exhausted him. The audience looked on, ashen-faced. "We have no idea precisely what this is. It doesn't match anything on file. None of the patients are developing any antibodies.

"Auerbach is currently being designated as the Index Case, our Patient Zero, although that may change as other reports come in. But the real problem is—it's already spread. The new reported cases aren't centered geographically around Auerbach. We have no hard data on how it's spreading nor on its ability to spread—although, to be fair, there's enough transporter traffic that if it got into a transporter and the biofilters don't catch it, it could be all over Sherman's."

Dr. Tyler called out from the gallery. "There's another 'but' there, John. I can hear it in your voice."

Ambrose looked up at the gallery. "Yes. Look around you, all of you. How many of your colleagues called in sick today? How many of you know people outside the hospital who are under the weather? How many of *you* are feeling it, too?"

A murmur went around the gallery.

"Yes. It's not just here. There's a twenty percent

absenteeism from schools today. I assume there are similar numbers in the workplace. Ladies and gentlemen, it is quite possible that we are all infected. Every last man, woman, and child on the planet."

Captain's Log, Stardate 53663.8.

I have invoked a planetary quarantine. No ship—nothing is getting on or off Sherman's Planet.

The planet's population has been over-come by a malady that Dr. Lense has taken to calling "Sherman's Plague." It is wildly conta-gious, and right now it appears that at least seventy percent of the planet is showing early symptoms of exposure. Five hundred and thirty-two people have shown advanced signs. We have reason to believe that it's quite possible that every human on the planet has been infected by it. It's not impossible that it's spread to every mammal. We honestly don't know yet.

What we do know is that things are chaotic on the planet surface. Many essential services were becoming short-staffed due to the illness, and now panic is setting in. Doctors and nurses are leaving hospitals. Local militias have been called up from reserves, a state of martial law has been declared by Planetary Administrator Orosz. All schools and businesses have been closed, transporter usage has been forbidden, people have been told to stay in their homes and rely on replicators. Most of our crew down on the planet has taken over running power stations, communications, computer systems, and security logistics, because so far they haven't been afflicted with symptoms. They're rising to the challenge, but I don't know how long thirty-five people can keep a colony of three and a half million people running.

Particularly hard hit has been the medical infrastructure of the planet. Due to the nature of the disease, the doctors and hospitals were at the front line treating the early cases, and so became very quickly infected themselves. People went to hospitals with the early symptoms, and the disease spread by proximity at an exponential rate. Nobody was expecting this, and according to Dr. Lense the incubation period must have been long enough so that by the time people noticed they were sick, everybody had it. There's almost nobody on the planet who can do anything. The front line of defense has been knocked out. And in any event, nobody is ever prepared for the entire population getting sick at the same time.

A few people have tried leaving the planet and running for help. Luckily, all of the folks who have tried have been in unarmed ships, and we've been able to keep them corralled.

It's kept Wong on his toes, flying after the strays and bringing them home. In some cases Hawkins has had to disable the ships first—with tractor beams mostly. In one case we actually had to open fire.

In a way, I've been lucky. Since Dr. Lense is still up here with me, she can still do work on the contagion. She's been getting as much information sent up to her as possible, and she's conducting all of the research on the problem via remote telemetry. She's somewhat limited as to what can be done, but she's doing the best she can. Her biggest problem is that sooner or later anybody on the planet who's acting on her behalf will themselves be too ill to help her. I've got some of the crew trying to set up EMHs in the hospitals, and Nurse Wetzel and Medtech Copper are helping where they can as well.

Which leads to the personal aspect of the problem: every member of my crew down there is also probably infected—certainly all the humans. They've got about a two-week lag behind everybody else on the planet, but they too will succumb to the disease if we can't find a solution to the problem. Even if they survive, if we can't find a way to disinfect them, I may be forced to keep them down there for the rest of their lives. Surrounded by corpses. And we have no idea what effect, if any, the disease will have on a Nasat or a Bynar or a Bolian or a Bajoran or on any of the other alien species represented on the *da Vinci.*

I'm off to sickbay to check in with Dr. Lense. She's said that she should have some results by now, so that we'll have some idea what we're up against here.

CHAPTER
4

"Okay, what do we know so far?" Gold asked. He was seated in one of the two guest chairs in Lense's tiny office in sickbay. Fabian Stevens sat in the chair next to her.

"It's a viral hemorrhagic fever, Captain," the doctor said. "It's a severe multisystem syndrome, like yellow fever, ebola, or Vulcan bebonea, but this is one we've never seen before."

Lense tapped on her padd, and a picture popped up on the screen behind her of an enlarged virus, along with chemical formulations.

"As near as I can determine, this is the pathogen."

Gold couldn't make heads or tails of the image, but commanding engineers for so long, he had grown accustomed to technobabble and the need to prompt specialists into using lay language. "Tell us how it works, what it does."

"Okay. It's spread as an aerosol. It's incredibly small, anything small enough to filter it out would make it impossible to breathe through. It appears to be robust enough to survive outside a human body for hours. It's prolific—apparently it's sticking very well to pollen and dust in the air and using that as a distribution aid. Contaminated clothing or bed linens could also spread the virus. The damn thing is more virulent than smallpox was. It attacks every cell in the body, except for brain tissue—and only because it kills the host before it can get that far. It appears to be causing a hemorrhaging in the lungs, making people drown in their own bodily fluids. Since it's also respired, it's exhaled into the open and spreads quickly from there. The virus appears first to target rapidly reproducing cells, like the lining of the trachea."

"Why the trachea?" asked Stevens.

"Because it's constantly irritated by breathing, coughing, what have you. In fact, that makes it worse, because the coughing helps make it airborne and contributes to the speed of spread. It also does a wonder on the stomach lining." She pulled up an image of an outline of a body, and pointed at the throat. "Gravity and eating just pull it along. It can incorporate into the DNA of those cells and live there, becoming part of every cell that forms when that cell and its progeny divide—"

"Exponential growth."

"Yes, Captain. Once there's enough of a viral load, it spreads to the rest of the body."

"How long does it take to work?" Gold asked.

"The incubation period appears to be about three weeks, then non-pulmonary symptoms start

to show up. Before that, all you'll see is a cough
and a sore throat. Our people showed up at the
tail end of the incubation period—pure bad timing."

"Could've been worse," Stevens interjected. "A
few days earlier, and we could've been out of here
carrying the infection to the entire galaxy. A week
later, and we might not have been able to help at
all."

Gold shrugged. "How does the timing affect our
people on the ground?"

"At this point, they've had the disease incubat-
ing for about three days. It'll be two weeks before
symptoms become evident. I can try vaccinating
our crew and that might lessen the effect, but
that's making the assumption that I can come up
with a vaccine that will work. They're probably a
week to ten days after the initial spread. In a few
days, they might be the only people on the planet
who can stand. And, of course, that's only the
humans—I can't even begin to guess how to treat
the nonhumans."

"How did it spread?"

"Not a clue. Because of the speed of spread, I
think we just got a random mutation that developed. I honestly don't know. There are probably
other non-sentient species that may be carrying it
as well, though I don't have the resources to tell
which yet. At least it doesn't seem to jump to
plants."

"Where did it come from?" Stevens asked.

"I don't know, and I don't really have the time to
find out. It might have been something old,

though, or it could've been brought on a cargo ship by accident or it could be a combination."

Gold nodded. "We're already checking on all ships that have been to Sherman's Planet in the last month—luckily, it's not that many. They're being kept in quarantine, and some of them are heading back here. So far, no one on them has shown symptoms."

"Fine. My first priorities are managing patients infected or suspected of being infected, and developing diagnostic tools."

"Agreed. So what can we do about it?"

"Right now, we're limited to supportive therapies—balancing the patient's fluids and electrolytes, maintaining their oxygen status and blood pressure, treating them for any complicating infections. You've already declared a quarantine, so that stops any interplanetary spread."

Gold exhaled long and hard and asked the question he didn't want to ask but needed some kind of answer for. "What's the mortality rate?"

"No way to tell, sir. So far, we've had a large number of people die from this thing . . . but I have no way to be absolutely sure until I see how many people actually can recover from it."

"How many do you expect?"

"Based on what I've seen so far, and the computer models I've run—I don't know if anybody is going to be able to survive at all."

The room was silent except for the usual background hum of the *da Vinci*'s impulse engines. Gold recovered first. "All right, Doctor, what can we do to help?"

"Do you know anything about molecular biology?"

"Um . . . no."

"Diagnostics? Clinical medicine, epidemiology, proteomics, immunology, pathogenesis, comparative biology, ecology, public health practices? Either of you?"

Stevens looked at Gold, then back at Lense sheepishly. "I can fake . . . some of it. Maybe."

"Then there's damn little you can do. You don't fake this. I get to do it all."

"No, you don't. Doctor, you've been running at warp eleven on all this. Go back to your quarters for six hours and take a break."

"There's no time, Captain. Forget it."

"Four hours."

"One hour."

"Two. That's an order."

She glared and took a deep breath. "All right. Two hours. Let me get Fabian up to speed and then I'll go. In the meantime, you keep on the horn and see what you can do about getting any other help here. I'm already transmitting what data I can to Starfleet Medical, but the lag time is way too long; they're useless."

"Fine. In the meantime, I'll see what I can do about keeping the ship running with a single op—"

"Don't try and one-up me, Captain, I'm not in the mood."

Gold shot Lense a look. "I'm not, Doctor—and I don't appreciate your tone or your assumption. Clear?"

Not waiting for an answer, Gold left the sickbay. Lense leaned back in her chair.

Stevens turned and looked at Lense. "Okaaay . . . now what can I do?"

Lense called out. "Emmett!"

The EMH materialized five feet in front of her. "Good morning, Doctor."

"We've got us a doozy, Emmett. Synch with my files and notes from the last forty-eight hours."

"Synching—oh."

"It's an epidemic. No, scratch that, it's a pandemic. We've just identified the pathogen, we're running tests to see what we can do to kill it. Keep an eye on the tests that are still running. He"—she pointed at Stevens—"is your extra set of hands. I'm going to get some rest, I've been told I need it."

The door opened to the cabin Lense shared with Domenica Corsi. Like the rest of the ship, it was quiet and empty. No noise in the hall, no chatter, just the constant background hum of the engines.

"Lights, one quarter." The room dimmed to a point that Lense could tolerate. The silence, however, would get to her. "Computer, play Vivaldi's *Four Seasons*."

The sounds of an orchestra filled the room and Lense collapsed into a chair. She massaged her temples, trying to relieve some of the eyestrain.

The computer beeped. *"You have a message from Lt. Commander Corsi."*

A message? That's not like her, Lense thought. She opened her eyes—there was no music. She must have fallen asleep in her chair and slept through the entire piece. "Computer, time?"

"The time is now fourteen hundred hours, twelve minutes."

She did some quick math in her head—she'd been asleep a little over two hours. "Tea, semihot, extra sugar, lemon, and caffeine." The replicator hummed and she took the suddenly appearing mug in her hands and sipped. "Play the message." She turned to the viewscreen on the wall, but there was no picture, just audio.

"Hey, roomie. I know we're both incredibly busy, with me trying to keep things running smoothly down here and you playing with your test tubes. I'm down at the spaceport—we're keeping the lid on. There are a lot of people who are trying to find a way off the planet, and I have my hands full keeping the ships grounded. I don't want to distract you, so you'll get this message when you get it. No rush—if you get it and it's necessary, there'll be plenty of time.

"From what I understand, there's a chance that I may be stuck on this planet for a very long time, either living out the rest of my days here or just taking up a good two meters of it. I'm not worried about it. I know you're doing your damnedest up there, but we've all gotta go sometime. But there is one important thing you've gotta do for me.

"If I don't make it off this planet, I want to make sure that my little brother gets the axe. It's a family heirloom, been in the family for years and years and years. He always complained that I got it. It's under my bed—I never found a good way to hang it on the wall. He's on Cestus III, living in Pike City, his

name's Roberto. You'll find—Get back here, you!"
Lense heard a sudden scuffle of background noise
and wondered just what was going on down there.

*"Got to get back to the situation at hand. You
have to get the axe to Bobby, or I'll haunt you from
one end of the galaxy to the other. And don't worry
about me. If I had to, I'd have commandeered a
shuttlecraft to get down here and do my job. This is
what I'm supposed to be doing, just like you're
doing what you have to do. Corsi out."*

Terrific, thought Lense. *Somebody else haunting
me. Just what I needed.*

She thought about Domenica Corsi, a woman
whom she'd shared a cabin with for a year and
knew almost nothing about. *Yes, but nobody
knows anything about her. Except maybe Fabian.*

Her eyes drifted to the drawers under Corsi's
bed. *The axe? What was that all about? Knowing
Core Breach, it's probably some old Klingon cleaver,
designed to slay seven* targs *with one blow.*

She got down and knelt in front of Corsi's bed,
then opened the drawers.

She didn't see it at first—then she saw a wooden
case about a meter long, in the back under some
civilian clothes. She emptied the drawer so she
could get at it, and took it out.

It was wood, but it had been sealed with a fixa-
tive; she couldn't feel the wood grain. It had a clear
top, and through it she could see the axe.

It wasn't a Klingon axe at all. It looked like it
was human made, and apparently very old—the
handle was made of wood and it was beginning to
show signs of age. The axe head rested on what

looked like a triangular pillow, a deep blue with white stars on it, and showed wear on the red paint. This was no ceremonial weapon; it had been used.

And down at the bottom of the case on the glass, there was a brass plaque. The inscription read:

> *A firefighter performs*
> *only one act of bravery in his life,*
> *and that's when he takes the oath.*
> *Everything he does after that*
> *is merely in the line of duty.*
> *In Memoriam—September 11, 2001*

Lense knew the date, and realized what she had to be holding.

She reverently placed the box down on Corsi's unmade bed, then turned and left to go back to sickbay.

Captain's Personal Log, Stardate 53665.1.

Things are not going well here. The number of advanced cases on the planet has cracked two thousand. The death toll is a hundred and thirteen. Dr. Lense is getting more and more frustrated and tense. I went to visit her in sickbay, and I saw her sitting at her desk working, while Emmett was running around from table to table, with numerous test tubes in his hands.

She's getting heavily stressed.

I realize this is a crucible issue for Dr. Lense—she's being placed in yet another life-or-death situation, where she is the last, best hope to save the lives of thousands upon thousands of people. Again. She had to do it during the war and failed—or rather, she didn't live up to her and everybody else's superhuman expectations—and now she's in a situation where the number of potential corpses could increase by three orders of magnitude from the last time.

And I don't have any way to take the burden off her. Deep Space Station K-7 is the closest help, and it's a week away. She's on her own.

I wonder what I'm actually going to put in the official log about all this.

CHAPTER
5

The doors to sickbay opened, and Fabian poked his head in. He saw that Dr. Lense was running between tables and screens and cultures, with Emmett following behind trying to keep up, but moving slowly and jerkily, like an internal motor was misfiring. "Hi, Doc. Can I play through, or is this a bad time?"

"Is there any way in which this could be construed as a good time, Fabian?"

"Hey, you've still got your health . . ." Fabian winced at his own stupid comment.

"Shut up. What do you need?"

"I need to put monitoring taps on Emmett's program. I'm worried about the load on his system, what with his database being accessed by a thousand different people. The degradation could get bad."

"Yes, I've noticed a lag in his performance too. Isn't there anything that can be done about that?"

"Not yet. The problem is the constant file

synching, and Emmett just wasn't designed for it. In theory, the main computers on the planet are better equipped, but they're short-handed—"

"Yes, yes. Do whatever you have to. Take processing power from all the other systems; we're the only ones up here and what we're doing is more important." She went back to staring at the screen, glancing over at flasks that Fabian could only conjecture about.

But it wasn't his concern. His was getting Emmett's program to scale upward so he could surpass his design specs by a thousandfold. He didn't want to tell her that he'd already cut back on every drain of excess CPU cycles he could think of. The *da Vinci* was practically running on a hamster on a wheel at this point.

"How goes the battle?" he asked.

"Badly. This thing is brutal. It'd be tough to design a more perfect pathogen against any humanoid race."

"That bad?"

"Worse. This thing attacks any organism that uses a nucleic acid as its genetic basis. Doesn't matter if it's DNA, RNA, or some of the more exotic forms, this virus has proteins that integrate into them all. And our vain hope that Pattie, Soloman, and the other nonhumans would be immune is fading. They're probably all just as vulnerable."

Fabian smiled wryly. "Wow. The holy grail of computing."

"Pardon me?"

"Sorry. Old computer problem, how to integrate data between nonstandard systems."

"How do computer engineers solve the problem?"

"Wait two years and upgrade the entire system."

"We don't have two years to wait here."

"Well, computer viruses don't give you the option either."

"Whatever." Lense went back to her monitor. She started muttering, probably to herself, though Fabian couldn't help overhear. "The hell of it is, I know that the virus would probably burn itself out in a week if it didn't have a live host—but that's every human on the planet."

Fabian piped up. "Shouldn't the transporter biofilters be taking the viruses out?"

Lense just kept staring at the screen and tapping. Fabian was sure he heard a growl.

"No, I guess not," Fabian said, after thinking about it a moment. "We could take out the airborne viruses, I suppose, but we couldn't do anything for the viruses already in the person's—wait a minute! Why can't we use the biofilters to take out the viruses in people's blood?"

"Because it's getting into the DNA of cells, including blood cells. That's what viruses do. We might be able to reduce the viral load of some patients, but it's a stopgap measure at best that would have to be applied to the entire population, and that's tough with three and a half million people."

"Damn. And it sounded so good."

Lense sighed. "Welcome to my life."

"Okay, we couldn't do anything for the viruses already in the person's DNA, and they'd just stay sick. And they'd keep pumping out the virus. And even if we could, the air on the planet is so saturated they just get reinfected. We couldn't keep them all up here while we clean up the planet, and we couldn't make an oxygen tent the size of a city."

"Mmm." Lense had gotten up and was looking at another batch of lab equipment. There'd been little indication that she'd heard a word he said.

Fabian continued talking out loud. "I guess fixing a human virus is a lot like fixing a computer virus."

"I doubt that." She spoke without looking up.

"No, I don't think they're that dissimilar. Correct me if I'm wrong, but when we fix the damage from an infected computer system, we have to go in and cut out the virus coding, repair the damaged files and data, and then program the system to recognize the virus in the future and not let it infect the system again."

"Yes. But the problem remains, what do you do when the data is so horribly corrupted that no recovery is possible?"

"Hope that you've made a backup recently."

"That's my problem. The virus has pretty much totaled every biological backup, all the places where there would be an uninfected strand of DNA to work with."

"Oh."

She looked at the screen. "And this thing just eats up cells. The human immune system isn't designed to handle viruses, it primarily targets proteins. It certainly isn't set up to handle this sort of thing."

"Yep. Sounds like it's time for a systems upgrade."

"If only—say that again."

"Say what again?"

"It's time for a systems upgrade."

"It's time for a systems upgrade. What about it?"

Lense stayed very still for ten seconds. Then she almost attacked her combadge. "Lense to Gold."

"Gold here. What is it?"

"Get down to sickbay. We have a solution!"

Captain's Personal Log, Stardate 53665.8.

Dr. Lense had just called me from sickbay, claiming she had worked out a cure to Sherman's Plague. I went down there to be briefed.

TRANSCRIPT BEGINS

G: Doctor?

L: Come in, come in! I've got it. It came to me in a flash. I'm working out the details of it now.

G: Where's Stevens off to? I just passed him in the hall.

L: I sent him ahead to start the work on the transporters. He's going to have to keep them running hot for probably at least thirty-six hours straight to handle the load. He wants to make sure they're ready as soon as I have it ready.

G: For what?

L: For the cure to work. It's going to take a couple of engineering tricks to get everything going, but—

G: Whoa, whoa, slow down. From the beginning, and with the small words?

L: We've got a way around it. Sherman's Plague just cuts through the human immune system like it wasn't there. The immune system was never designed to handle something like this. So we're building a new immune system. I'm writing the DNA sequences now. Thank heaven the planet is almost entirely human stock. I don't want to think about the time it would take to write multiple versions of the enzymes. Good thing the last organ affected is the brain—if not, even when we fixed the virus you'd lose memory and learned behavior, because those cells would be destroyed . . . .

G: Wait a minute. Explain to me what you're doing.

L: Okay, it's something like this. I've developed a few potential cures here, all variations on the same theme. First is DNA that we'll append directly to the cells of the infected—not too hard. The new sequences will go in and respond directly to Sherman's Plague, preventing it from causing any more damage.

We have a series of steps. Step one

we've already done, figuring out what's causing this and how it works. Step two: identify the viral DNA sequences in every infected cell in a body. Step three: remove those sequences and rejoin the human DNA, making repairs and restoring to the original as closely as possible. Step four: cause the immune system to recognize the virus and prevent it from reinfecting the cells. Step five: repair the damage on a tissue level rather than cellular, restoring organ function and what have you. Step six: eliminating the virus from the environment, so this plague never happens again. Step one is already done. Step two and three go together. We need an enzyme complex—

G: Pardon?

L: Think natural nanotech.

G: Got it.

L: The enzyme complex needs to be able to read the DNA of the chromosomes and recognize the viral sequences. Luckily, the virus doesn't change its own DNA sequences—if it did, the problem would be almost unsolvable. Once it finds a viral sequence, it needs to excise it and degrade it, then it needs to rejoin the organism's own DNA, which was interrupted by the virus. Fortunately, we don't have to design this enzyme complex from scratch, we're going to use off-the-shelf parts.

G: What parts?

L: The basic structure is a ribosome, which is a normal part of a cell that turns RNA into proteins. We're recoding it to recognize this particular viral sequence.

G: Go on.

L: Then we're going to attach a DNA endonuclease, which is part of the normal DNA repair machinery that prevents mutations by removing pieces of DNA. And then we add a ligase, which will glue the two ends back together.

G: Step four?

L: Step four . . . the virus is designed—

G: Designed? This was deliberate?

L: Sorry. Bad choice of terms. The virus protects itself by turning off the ability of the immune system to recognize and destroy it, like most viruses. Adenovirus does it all the time.

G: Never heard of it.

L: The common cold.

G: We cured that, didn't we?

L: Stop interrupting, please. We need to duplicate an immune system, with modifications so that the virus is unable to shut it off.

G: A nontrivial problem.

L: Yes. But again, we're working with off-the-shelf parts and building on them.

G: Step five, we already know how to do.

L: Once the virus is removed so no further

damage is caused, yes. Simple, if we can
do it in time. Our factors are time and
the sheer number of patients that have
to be treated. We're going to tap every
available resource to pull that off.

G: And step six?

L: Wiping it out in the ecosystem. Getting
the population immune will help effect
that, as the virus then will have no place
to live. My guess is that it will burn out
on its own in about two months. We can
improve on those numbers by releasing
disassemblers into the air to break
down the airborne pathogen. Search
and destroy. We may also have to consider a controlled destruction of live-
stock, once we have an idea of what
other species this infects, if any.

G: Good. So when can we take the next
steps?

L: Very soon. I'm working on the precise
identifiers now. So to do all this, we're
going to have to add a forty-seventh
chromosome.

G: What?

L: No way around it. It's a gigantic amount
of data and this is the only way to do it.
What we'll have to set up is a sort of
triage. First, we're going to have to run
the most critical cases through the
main transporter and add the chromosome directly to their DNA when we
rematerialize them. At the same time,

we're going to be using the cargo transporters as long-distance replicators,
seeding the atmosphere of the planet
with an artificial virus as widely as possible, which implants the chromosome.
We hook it to helper cells, which will
allow the virus to quickly reproduce,
with limits so that it can't reproduce
without the helper cells. Once they get
into the air, they should multiply and
spread, infecting the rest of the population with the cure, which should propa-
gate through the body in the next forty-
eight hours or so. We're going to have to
get all of our people into environmental
suits, as they're still early enough in the
stages that a full genetic rewrite probably won't be necessary for them for
another few days, so that should give us
enough time. At least I hope not, I'm not
positive yet if I'll be able to pull this off
on the nonhumans. We'll have to beam
them up to the ship so they can eat and
the like, but we can do that—somebody's going to have to spell Fabian at
the transporters after a while anyway.

G: And this is all that you've got?

L: What do you mean, "this is all that
you've got?" It'll work. It's our best shot.

G: I see. Doctor, I'm afraid I have to say
no. You can't do it. You can't perform
the procedure. Federation law is very
clear on this point.

L: Excuse me?

G: DNA resequencing and genetic tampering is strictly forbidden, except in cases of serious birth defects. Find another way.

L: There is no other way, Captain. This is it.

G: There has to be an alternative to genetically reengineering the entire population of a planet. Can't we genetically modify the virus itself?

L: We could have if we'd gotten here early enough, but it's already in everybody's system. The damage is already done.

G: What about having the transporter remove the virus itself?

L: Not an option either. It would take far too long to have the computers go through and check for the damage from the virus, and it might introduce errors into the rematerialization. It's much easier to add the chromosome, and then have it do the necessary work. Besides, your version is genetic modification as well.

G: What does Emmett say?

L: He has no valid opinion.

G: How can he have no valid opinion? How can you say that?

L: He has no valid opinion. His programming won't account for it; there's nothing in there about proscribed procedures. He seems to be unable even to consider it. We tried running it past him and he said he was unable to perform the procedure.

G: That settles it. It's not going to be done.

L: No, Captain. You don't have a valid medical opinion either.

G: I beg your pardon?

L: You have no idea as to what can or can't be done, what should or should not be done. The only thing you're willing to put faith in is what people in a little office on the other side of the galaxy are dictating to you.

G: No negotiation, Doctor. This is what you have to do. Do it by the book.

L: You're an idiot. I can't believe I'm hearing this. You're being a fool.

G: You're not a free agent in this. You're lucky that you are allowed to practice medicine at all right now.

L: Oh, really?

G: Yes. I'm sorry, but—

L: Computer. Voice ID, Doctor Elizabeth Lense.

C: Voice ID confirmed.

L: Captain David Gold is becoming agitated and overwrought, and is showing signs of clear cognitive difficulties. Under Starfleet Medical Regulation 121, Section A, I am preparing to relieve him of command.

G: What?!

L: Emmett, activate. Wake up.

EMH: Good afternoon, Doctor.

G: Doctor—

L: The captain is becoming very agitated. Prepare a sedative—two ccs of damitol.

G: What do you think you're doing?

L: I may need your assistance in restraining him, Emmett. Don't hurt him—he's obviously confused. Possibly delusional.

G: Dear God, you're serious.

L: Serious as a mass grave. Which is what I'm going to have if I don't get back to work here.

G: Don't be a *putz*, Doctor. I can't let you do this.

L: Let me put it to you in simple, easy-to-understand words, Captain. There is a plague ravaging the population of the planet below us. I am the closest thing to a functioning medical authority within a light year, which makes every person down there my patient. I have prescribed a regimen of treatment which, according to my ability and judgment, I consider for the best benefit of my patients. And I have a person up here who is attempting to prevent me from saving their lives.

G: I want their lives saved, too, but you're mutating them!

L: You see? You don't even know what I'm doing. You have no idea. All you can do is help me do this or get out of my way. You can't do it by yourself.

G: Doctor, I would be very careful if I were you. This is mutiny. Comput—

L: Shush shush shush. Understand me, Captain. You need me right now a lot more than I need you. Because I guarantee you, if you don't let me do this, *your* career will be over. I will report to the board of inquiry that you overrode the advice of your ship's medical officer, and as a result, allowed millions of sentient beings to die needlessly. Your career—no, your *life* will be over. I can do it with or without you, Captain, and frankly at this point I don't care which. You can't do it without me.

I can save lives here, Captain, and by God I will *not* let you or some silly law prevent me from doing that. Now, are you going to take responsibility for what's going to happen, or am I?

Captain, it's going to take me at least an hour before I can start applications. I have to finish designing the resequencing enzymes and run them through computer modeling, and Fabian has to finish rewiring the transporters. I have work to do either way, so you have an hour to make up your mind. With or without you, Captain. In the meantime, get out of my sickbay and let me work.

TRANSCRIPT ENDS

* * *

What else could I do? I left.

To be honest, arguing wasn't going to do anything but escalate the situation, and she might make good on her threat. And in any case, it would have wasted valuable time.

I believe her threat is not an idle one. There are only a few people on the ship now. She could certainly claim medical authority to have me removed from command, even temporarily, leaving her free to do whatever she was going to do anyway.

She has given me an hour to make a decision. But if this decision is going to be made, it's going to be made by rational people thinking it through, not because one stressed-out person blackmailed another into it. I do not cave in to blackmail.

I dislike having to essentially hand over command to a member of my crew because they have more relevant knowledge of the issue at hand than I do. Does that give them the right to usurp the center chair whenever they feel like it?

On the other hand, someone's got to drive. Shouldn't it be the best driver?

Ordinarily, yes. But what if you know that the driver is going to break laws?

Honestly, I'm less concerned about the laws being broken than I am about Lense being broken. Because, like it or not, she's the only option I have. And so I have to be extra careful about using her without breaking her.

So does that mean that I'm going along and indulging her power trip, even for a few minutes?

No. I want to save the population here as well. But the principles of the Prime Directive apply here. The Prime Directive says, basically, that we shouldn't tamper. Internally, the same concept guides our thinking on tampering with ourselves. The original impetus was in reaction to the Eugenics Wars, but the point is we do not have the right to alter our biology to such a radical extent that it gives such a huge evolutionary advantage. And that's what Dr. Lense is proposing here. To be given more than what we've been born with. If the laws regarding genetic enhancement were as inconsequential as she tried to make them out to be, she wouldn't have spent two months on Starbase 314 having her life pored over.

I can hear Rachel telling me, "God never gives anybody more than they can handle."

Actually, that's not what I'm hearing. The voice is not from the *shul*, it's from the kitchen. She was with our youngest granddaughter, Emily, who was visiting from Florida when she was seven. I came upon them in the kitchen, praying for snow. Emily had never seen the white stuff except for the holovids, and was looking to frolic. Rachel, even more so, to play with a granddaughter in the snow. She was even more excited than a seven-year-old. The only problem was it was the beginning of December, and I knew at that time of year the odds of getting snow in New York were almost nonexistent. And I told them so, and that praying for snow was a dumb idea.

Rachel looked at me, then at Emily. And she said, "What could it hurt?"

Okay. We're out of all other options to save the people down there. Lense can't or won't deliver another option. The death toll is rising. Lense knows the consequences to herself of her actions, and she's determined to go ahead and do it anyway.

What could it hurt?

All right, we've established that we'll go ahead and do it. Now how can I help Dr. Lense? Play manager here, David. She's determined to go through with her plan. My question is, how can I help her? How can I make it easier for her? Heck, how can I help us both avoid prison time?

CHAPTER
6

Dr. Lense was running among three different terminals, checking the progress of the sims. She had set up simulations of the modified DNA sequences, and was now testing them against DNA records of various human genotypes to determine if they would actually work in the field.

The first set of results had not been encouraging, and had forced Lense to lose a half hour, time she was acutely aware of. She knew that the deaths would plot out over time like a bell curve, and knew that with every minute wasted she was beginning to ascend the curve. She imagined a grisly pile of corpses, piling up higher and higher in the shape of a bell curve . . . .

"Gold to sickbay."

The interruption snapped her out of her reverie. "Whatever it is, make it quick. I'm busy."

"Doctor, I need a quick medical opinion. Would you concur that not being able to survive in the

ecosystem one was born in would be considered a
severe birth defect in the individual?"

Lense blinked, then answered slowly. "Yes. Yes,
it would."

"Then I must concede that you are acting to cor-
rect a severe and widespread birth defect in the pop-
ulation of Sherman's Planet. I will so note in the
official log and all reports I make to Starfleet on this
matter."

Lense almost fumbled the petri dish in her
hand.

"Congratulations, Doctor. You have my blessing
for a go-ahead. I'm on board with you—we'll deal
with the legal ramifications later."

"If it helps, I've set up the forty-seventh chromosome with their own marker tags. We'll probably be able to flush them out of people's systems
later, after we've determined that the plague is out
of the atmosphere."

"Probably, she says."

"Medicine isn't an exact science, Captain."

"You're not doing a very good job of reassuring
me, Doctor. How soon can your crazy plan be imple-
mented?"

"Give me another ten minutes. The initial
sequences didn't work out; I'm running simulations on the latest batch now. You can start checking in on the rest of the crew up here, and see if
they're going to be ready to go when I am."

"Will do. Gold out."

Lense exhaled. She didn't realize how much of
her breath she had been holding. "Sickbay to
Stevens."

"Go ahead, Doc."

"How soon are you going to be ready?"

"Cargo transporters are done. I'm finishing final tweaks on the mains. Diego's been consulting over the coms and whimpering a lot, but we're actually ahead of schedule here."

"Good. Get ready, I'm going to have specs for you in a bit." She turned to Emmett. "How are you doing on the airborne antivirus?"

"I believe we have it completed and ready for testing."

"Now we're cooking. Upload them to Stevens. Fabian!"

"Yes, ma'am?"

"You've got a file coming to you from Emmett. Feed that into the cargo transporters and go!"

"Reading the file—got it. And it's loaded into the transporter buffers. And now, with a wave of my little magic wa—"

"Just run it! I've got too many other things to do!"

"You take all the fun out of things. Energizing!"

"Stevens to bridge. Captain, you should be seeing the first transports now on the big board, if you want. I'm headed to the main transporter room now."

"Let's take a look. Wong, put it up on screen. Zoom in."

"Aye, sir." A picture of the planet's surface directly below the ship appeared on the bridge's main viewscreen, about a hundred square kilometers' worth. In the atmosphere of the planet, a transporter twinkle started appearing on the planet in a grid pattern—barely seen from high above, it was a thousand points of light blinking in and out, flickering all over the place.

"Okay," said Gold, "it's a start."

"Okay," said Lense, "it's a start. Now comes the hard part. Fabian, how's it going?"

"Not too bad. Just waiting to hear from—"

"Duffy to Stevens," said the new voice over the com channel.

"Stevens here. How's it going down there, Duff?"

"The pattern enhancers are in place around the worst cases down here, Fabe."

"Cases? Plural?"

"Yeah, Docto—oh, damn. We can't do it that way? The genetic patterns will get mixed up?"

"No, it should work when we're doing it *en masse*, we should be able to do six at a time. But for my initial tests, I need one."

"Then we can calibrate off that," Fabian added.

"Okay, hang on." There was a pause, then a beep. *"I just placed my combadge on a patient here. Can you get a lock on her?"*

"Scanning—got it."

"Make sure you've got all the medical equipment with her."

"Tha-a-a-ank you, Duff, I knew that. We're ready to energize. Doctor?"

Lense stood in sickbay, not moving for five seconds. Had she forgotten anything? She was sure she'd covered everything, and she had to test it somewhere. "Wait, Fabian. I want to be there and see the patient," she said as she walked toward the door.

"You won't be able to interact with her. She'll be behind a force field, to prevent contamination."

She had already reached the turbolift. "I know. But I want to see her for myself. Deck five."

"All right. We're holding here."

"Thank you. Be there in a few seconds. Lense out."

Lense sprinted from the turbolift down the corridor to the main transporter room. Stevens was at the console when she came in, and a shimmering force field wall had been erected in front of the transporter platform.

"Ready to go?" Stevens asked.

She took out a tricorder. "Ready. Let's do it."

Fabian nodded. "All right, here we go. Energizing."

He moved his hands across the console, and the familiar hum started. On the platform, a woman appeared on a sickbed. Lense looked at the woman, and she was already beginning to fade—Fabian had programmed the transporter to immediately cycle back and forth. The patient was elderly, Lense estimated her age at around one hundred twenty from what she could see, but the years had not diminished her stare. She caught Lense's eye just before she completely winked out.

"She's back here," Duffy said over the com.

"Confirmed," Stevens said.

"Are they in her?" Lense asked.

"Yup, no problems. The extra chromosome has

been systematically added to every cell in her body. Are we going to wait and see how she took it?"

"No time. I wish there was, but—"

"Right, I understand."

Stevens nodded. "I think we can start going for multiple transports, then. Duff, how you set up down there?"

"Ready to roll, Fabe. We're tagging the worst cases and transmitting their frequencies to you."

"Great. Executing transporter cycling program Stevens-9 now." Fabian's hands flashed over the console, and the transporter platform filled with six patients and sickbeds—then they disappeared, to be replaced by another six. Here, then not, here, then not, over and over again in a slow motion strobing effect. It was entrancing.

Lense looked over at Stevens, who was concentrating on the console and muttering under his breath. She got closer to listen, and heard him saying, "Yes, happy to see you here . . . no waiting, we'll be right with you . . . just leave your payments up front . . . take two of these and call us in the morning . . . "

Lense reached over tentatively and touched his arm. Stevens half-glanced down where she touched him, but went on with his tasks and mutterings. "Yes, turn your head and cough . . . Feeling run-down? By what?"

She hugged him then.

Stevens didn't respond, he just kept on working.

She let go and turned to leave, and saw Captain Gold standing quietly in the back of the room. She missed him entirely—had he been there when she

rushed in, or did he come in during all the excitement? She started to speak, but Gold held a finger
to his lips, then pointed to the door.

The two of them walked out together.

Captain's Personal Log, Stardate 53670.1.

The worst of it all has passed.

It's been two weeks since we released the
antiviral regimen. We've been able to halt the
spread of Sherman's Plague. No new cases
have been reported in the last ten days. We
repaired much of the damage to the population. Fatalities have been, all things considered, very few—we couldn't save about a half
a percent of the population, they were too
far gone. We also had to destroy a portion
of the animal population, much to our regret.
Luckily, this is a planet that remembers
famines, and has prepared for it. And none of
the grains were poisoned, so that's a help.

The real problems have been the sec-
ondary effects from lack of services, but
Gomez, Corsi, and Duffy have been working
long and hard to get them back up to snuff.

Everybody is back on the ship. Gomez has
requested that the next time I suggest com-
bining an assignment with a shore leave, I
should consider building a hot tub for the
Founders' homeworld.

And then there's Dr. Lense. I ordered her to
bed right after they started the transporter

therapy—I told her that right now, the only thing to be doing was waiting, and I could do that as well as she could, but I couldn't catch up on sleep for her. She slept for twenty hours, then she jumped right back into the fray, checking on reports from the planet, seeing how patients were responding, and commandeering the ship's sensors to track the spread of the antivirus.

She took to the authority much better than I thought she would have. We talked about it, in what I believe will be the last conversation with her I will have to record.

TRANSCRIPT BEGINS

G: Come.

L: Good afternoon, Captain.

G: Good afternoon, Doctor. Water for you? Something to nosh on?

L: Tangerine juice, if you don't mind.

G: Here you go.

L: Thank you. I have the final report on the crew. We were able to keep all of our crew free of the cure virus. As we suspected, many of them were indeed infected, a few weren't. I'm still trying to figure out why. I suspect a different regime of childhood vaccinations. But it'll take a while to figure out.

G: So we've seen the last of Sherman's Plague?

L: Except for two test tubes full of it.

One's down there, in the main medical facility. The other's up here in
sickbay.

G: High-level containment fields?

L: No, a jar on my desk. I'm saving it for
the holiday party.

G: Cute. Does that mean we're ready to
release the . . . what would you call it, a
counter-chromosome?

L: Already in the works. I want another
forty-eight hours, then we can release it.

G: And there should be no side effects
from that?

L: None whatsoever.

G: I'm glad to hear it. Speaking of which,
I've heard back from Starfleet Head-
quarters.

L: How nice to hear from my favorite people in the quadrant. And what do they
have to say for themselves?

G: They're happy to hear that Sherman's
Plague has been contained. They're
none too thrilled about your methods;
however, they're willing to accept our
interpretation of the statutes regarding
genetic engineering.

L: Remind me again. What story are we
using?

G: Don't be droll. They still want to punish
you for breaking the regs.

L: Ah, yes. Demerits for a job well done.

G: It's nothing to make light of. I think
there are some who wanted your com-

mission, your medical license, and your scalp. Not necessarily in that order.

L: So why aren't they doing it?

G: Well, there was also a big push from about three million people whose lives you saved that said otherwise. It seemed easier to accept our take on the situation than cause an incident.

L: "An incident"? Captain, I've seen some of the opinion columns down there. My favorites were, "we should say we've become more genetically enhanced than we really are and scare them into letting us have our way" and "let's drop a beaker of Sherman's Plague into San Francisco Bay and see how they like it."

G: Well, that's the story and we're sticking to it. Starfleet doesn't want a wholesale revision of the laws surrounding genetic engineering.

L: And why not? I've recently come to the conclusion that those laws could use a good reexamination.

G: In any event, *Doctor*, if Starfleet really wanted to take your commission, I'm sure you could retire and live quite comfortably down on Sherman's Planet. I understand from Administrator Orosz that there's talk about them putting up statues of you.

L: Oh, good grief.

G: Doctor, you just saved the lives of everyone on the planet.

L: Almost. Not all of them.

G: No, not all. But saving ninety-nine-point-five percent of the population isn't chicken feed.

L: If you say so. Percentage wise, it's pretty good. In absolute numbers, that's 72,134 people—never mind.

G: I know. It's still a lot of people who died. But it's a lot more people who lived.

L: A statue, hmm? Are they sure they want a statue for the person who might get them kicked out of the Federation?

G: You saved their lives. I'd think anything after that is something they'd rather deal with than dying.

L: My point all along.

G: For what it's worth, I don't think the Federation is going to ask them to leave—they never have before. So they might be a bit healthier than the average human, so what?

L: Of course, there's never been a case like this before, where a society in the Federation completely reengineered itself.

G: True. But there's a first time for everything. I just don't want to think what might happen if a planet decided to do it without this sort of emergency—say, if the Bajorans decided to become stronger than the Jem'Hadar.

L: Speaking of first times for everything, how big is my statue going to be?

G: Oy. Have I just overinflated your ego?

L: I'm a doctor. Our egos are naturally overinflated.

G: I suppose that's what happens when you have that much pressure placed on you.

L: Simple hydraulics.

G: Occasionally, you do get blowouts. Or fast leaks.

L: Nothing some maintenance won't take care of.

G: I don't know how much more I can provide—I'd think you'd want to be handled by more professional psychiatrists, not an amateur like myself.

L: No, I think I'd like to keep coming for a while. Besides which, I really think you have a few issues of your own that need addressing—your feelings of alienation about being the hardcore Starfleet man among all the engineers, all of whom are far more advanced than you in their specialties, and thus you have to rely on them, undermining your authority over them.

G: I'm a Starfleet captain. Our egos are naturally overinflated, too. And unlike doctors, we don't get extra points for being humble either. Incidentally, Dr. Lense—don't ever pull that shtick of threatening my command again.

L: I'll make you a deal, Captain. You don't attempt to countermand me in my area of expertise, and I won't try to run the ship.

G: Such a deal.

L: I thought so. Though, to be fair, you do make a decent counselor. Not professional in any sense, but—

G: But good enough for a friend, Elizabeth?

L: Good afternoon, Captain.

G: Good afternoon, Doctor. You're welcome back at any time.

L: I'll be around. Thank you again for the juice.

TRANSCRIPT ENDS

I'm under no illusions that she's fully cured— I don't really have that big an ego. In fact, this recent lionization may have just exchanged one set of neuroses for another, from feelings of inadequacy to feelings of superiority and arrogance. However, at the very least she's functional again, so I'll take it as an improvement. But I will have to keep an eye on her.

I wonder what she meant by that "undermined authority" crack. I'll have to ask her about that next time.

ABOUT THE AUTHORS

A fifteen-year-plus veteran of comic books, **Mike Collins** has worked as writer and artist on many iconic characters, including Superman, Batman, Spider-Man, Judge Dredd, and the X-Men in both U.S. and British comics. However, Mike has been happiest writing and drawing *Star Trek* comics for the past decade for Marvel Comics, WildStorm, and the British comics weekly *TV21*. Outside of comics, Mike works in animation as a designer and storyboard artist, has contributed to Oxford University Press's English as a Second Language Book division, and various other educational-based graphic projects. He is currently writing and designing a major graphic novel (the first in Welsh) for the Welsh TV/Movie Company S4C, to accompany their film adaptation of the Welsh myth cycle *The Mabinogion*. He has also provided the covers for all the *S.C.E.* eBooks since *Interphase* Book 1. He lives in Cardiff, Wales, with his wife and three daughters, two cats and a dog, and a lot of *Star Trek* stuff.

Ian Edginton's first collaboration with fellow West Midlandser Mike Collins was on Marvel Comics' *Star Trek: Early Voyages* series. A comic-book writer of long standing, Ian has worked in the industry for well over a decade and has written for most of the popular mainstay comic book characters such as Batman, the X-Men, Blade, X-Force, and Spider-Man. He also specializes in working on licensed film and television characters, including amongst them *Xena: Warrior Princess*, *Star Wars*, *Star Trek*, and *The Terminator*. He has also written the comic book sequel to Tim Burton's re-imagining of the *Planet of the Apes* franchise. However, Ian's most substantial body of licensed work is in relation to the *Aliens* and *Predator* films, where he has contributed to both movie canons.

Robert Greenberger is no stranger to *Star Trek*, having edited the comic book version for eight years while at DC Comics. During his time there, his work included the graphic novel *Star Trek: Debt of Honor*, which earned several industry awards and was named one of the best *Star Trek* comics of all time at PsiPhi.org. Bob has also written numerous *Star Trek* books, several in collaboration with Peter David and/or Michael Jan Friedman. On his own, he wrote *The Romulan Stratagem* and most recently, the third installment in 2001's *Gateways* crossover series, *Doors into Chaos*. He also wrote the final chapter, "The Other Side," in the concluding volume, *What Lay Beyond*, and is presently working on another *Star Trek: The Next Generation* epic and another *S.C.E.* eBook. He has also written a small number of shorter works ranging from biographies of Wilt Chamberlain, Ponce de Leon, and Lou Gehrig to original fiction like the short story "A Matter of Faith" in 2002's *Oceans of Space*. Bob makes his home in Connecticut with his wife, Deb, and children, Kate and Robbie.

Glenn Hauman is a man of many talents and many more job prospects. He was in e-publishing back when most folks thought that they'd be delivered over floppy disks, and decided to finally write one instead of publishing them. He was an editorial consultant to Simon & Schuster Interactive for many years, contributing to the *Star Trek Encyclopedia*, *Star Trek: The Next Generation Companion* and *Star Trek: Deep Space Nine Companion*, and many other *Star Trek* CD-ROMs (and one *Farscape* one, just to be different). His X-Men short stories "On the Air" (*The Ultimate X-Men*) and "Chasing Hairy" (*X-Men Legends*) were featured on the Sci-Fi Channel's Seeing Ear Theater, and he's got another *S.C.E.* eBook in the works. He's given up on his cunning plan to add extra hours to the day, and is now trying to add the hours to the week, where there's more room. If he can pull that off, he promises to use the extra time to update his Web page so you can read an even longer version of his biography.

Jeff Mariotte has written over half a dozen novels and two nonfiction books (some in collaboration with other authors) set in the *Buffy the Vampire Slayer/Angel* universe, two collaborative novels about superhero team *Gen¹³*, and a great many comic books, including the critically acclaimed *Desperadoes*. As Senior Editor for WildStorm Productions, one of his responsibilities has been the *Star Trek* comic book line, and he's currently hard at work on a full-length novel as part of the *Star Trek: The Lost Era* miniseries. With his wife, Maryelizabeth Hart, and their partner, Terry Gilman, he is an owner of the specialty science fiction/fantasy/mystery bookstore Mysterious Galaxy (www.mystgalaxy.com) in San Diego. He lives in San Diego with his wife, two children, and two cats and a dog in a house full of books and toys, comics, music, and laughter.

Look for STAR TREK fiction from Pocket Books

Star Trek®

Star Trek: Deep Space Nine®

Enterprise®

Novelizations

Star Trek®: New Frontier

#5 • *Martyr* • Peter David
#6 • *Fire on High* • Peter David
The Captain's Table #5: Once Burned • Peter David
Double Helix #5: Double or Nothing • Peter David
#7 • *The Quiet Place* • Peter David
#8 • *Dark Allies* • Peter David
#9–11 • *Excalibur* • Peter David
    #9 • *Requiem*
    #10 • *Renaissance*
    #11 • *Restoration*
Gateways #6: Cold Wars • Peter David
Gateways #7: What Lay Beyond: "Death After Life" • Peter David
#12 • *Being Human* • Peter David

Star Trek®: Stargazer

The Valiant • Michael Jan Friedman
Double Helix #6: The First Virtue • Michael Jan Friedman and
    Christie Golden
Gauntlet • Michael Jan Friedman
Progenitor • Michael Jan Friedman

Star Trek®: Starfleet Corps of Engineers (eBooks)

Have Tech, Will Travel (paperback) • various
    #1 • *The Belly of the Beast* • Dean Wesley Smith
    #2 • *Fatal Error* • Keith R.A. DeCandido
    #3 • *Hard Crash* • Christie Golden
    #4 • *Interphase, Book One* • Dayton Ward & Kevin Dilmore
Miracle Workers (paperback) • various
    #5 • *Interphase, Book Two* • Dayton Ward & Kevin Dilmore
    #6 • *Cold Fusion* • Keith R.A. DeCandido
    #7 • *Invincible, Book One* • David Mack & Keith R.A.
DeCandido
    #8 • *Invincible, Book Two* • David Mack & Keith R.A.
DeCandido
    #9 • *The Riddled Post* • Aaron Rosenberg
    #10 • *Gateways Epilogue: Here There Be Monsters* • Keith R.A.
DeCandido
    #11 • *Ambush* • Dave Galanter & Greg Brodeur
    #12 • *Some Assembly Required* • Scott Ciencin & Dan Jolley
    #13 • *No Surrender* • Jeff Mariotte

#14 • *Caveat Emptor* • Ian Edginton & Mike Collins
#15 • *Past Life* • Robert Greenberger
#16 • *Oaths* • Glenn Hauman
#17 • *Foundations, Book One* • Dayton Ward & Kevin Dilmore
#18 • *Foundations, Book Two* • Dayton Ward & Kevin Dilmore
#19 • *Foundations, Book Three* • Dayton Ward & Kevin Dilmore
#20 • *Enigma Ship* • J. Steven and Christina F. York
#21 • *War Stories, Book One* • Keith R.A. DeCandido
#22 • *War Stories, Book Two* • Keith R.A. DeCandido
#23 • *Wildfire, Book One* • David Mack
#24 • *Wildfire, Book Two* • David Mack
#25 • *Home Fires* • Dayton Ward & Kevin Dilmore
#26 • *Age of Unreason* • Scott Ciencin
#27 • *Balance of Nature* • Heather Jarman

Star Trek®: Invasion!

#1 • *First Strike* • Diane Carey
#2 • *The Soldiers of Fear* • Dean Wesley Smith & Kristine Kathryn Rusch
#3 • *Time's Enemy* • L.A. Graf
#4 • *The Final Fury* • Dafydd ab Hugh
Invasion! Omnibus • various

Star Trek®: Day of Honor

#1 • *Ancient Blood* • Diane Carey
#2 • *Armageddon Sky* • L.A. Graf
#3 • *Her Klingon Soul* • Michael Jan Friedman
#4 • *Treaty's Law* • Dean Wesley Smith & Kristine Kathryn Rusch
The Television Episode • Michael Jan Friedman
Day of Honor Omnibus • various

Star Trek®: The Captain's Table

#1 • *War Dragons* • L.A. Graf
#2 • *Dujonian's Hoard* • Michael Jan Friedman
#3 • *The Mist* • Dean Wesley Smith & Kristine Kathryn Rusch
#4 • *Fire Ship* • Diane Carey
#5 • *Once Burned* • Peter David
#6 • *Where Sea Meets Sky* • Jerry Oltion
The Captain's Table Omnibus • various

Star Trek®: The Dominion War

Star Trek®: Section 31™

Star Trek®: Gateways

Star Trek® Omnibus Editions

Star Trek® Short Story Anthologies

Other Star Trek® Fiction